LYGOS

THE DISCARDED HEROES | A NOVELLA

RONIE KENDIG

TASK FORCE
p r e s s

Lygos
© 2017 by Ronie Kendig
Print Edition
ISBN 978-0-9981367-4-5

This book is a work of fiction. Names, characters, places, and incidents are either products of the author's imagination or used fictitiously. Any similarity to actual people, organizations, and/or events is purely coincidental.

For more information about Ronie Kendig, visit her: www.roniekendig.com

Ronie is represented by Steve Laube of The Steve Laube Agency

Cover design: Kirk DouPonce, DogEared Design

Printed in the United States of America.

ALSO BY RONIE KENDIG

CHAPTER 1

Somewhere in Turkey

KILLING SOMEONE CHANGED a person—irrevocably altered how they viewed life, each breath, and each day . . . or the next kill. It was in his blood, in his wiring. Every building he entered, road he traveled, had him scouting potential targets, possible enemies, quick exits. This long in the field left him with more adrenaline in his veins than blood. Risk was a habit, not an exception. A need.

Crack! Thwat!

He instinctively ducked at the sound of weapons fire.

"Lygos, 'bout time you lived up to that name." Pinned down across the street, Firethorn growled through the comms.

"Digitalis," came the voice of Max Jacobs—Nightshade Actual—through the comms, "you got anything?"

"No joy," Digitalis reported.

A sniper had taken the Nightshade team by surprise just as their five-man team was heading to extraction. With three of them pinned down, Azzan Yasir climbed out the window and slithered through the night. For most of his life, he'd slipped through streets and lives with none the wiser. Now, he did it to save men who had become his friends, his family. Men who'd welcomed him to their team and despite their other nicknames, had given him an official call sign to go with this position on the team: Lygos. The ancient name of a deadly poisonous plant. Just like the others on the team: Nightshade, Digitalis, Wolfsbane, and Firethorn. Maybe he fit in now.

In black tactical pants and shirt, Azzan crouched atop the building. A cool wind brushed the wool cap he'd donned as he planted a foot on the north ledge and another pointing east. He peered through the thermal goggles, drew an imaginary line of fire from the building to the direction from which the shot had come.

Although he could make out a shape, there was no heat signature. Easy enough to mask, though, so that didn't mean much. Except that this guy could be a pro.

Evens the playing field.

Light on his feet and stealthy, Azzan shoved up and over the ledge. Sailed through the air, onto the next roof. He rolled his landing to soften the sound and impact. He came up running and pitched himself at the plaster wall jutting from the roof. Nailed it with the balls of his feet and angled to the right. Straight at the shadows huddled in the corner where a missing chunk of the ledge provided the perfect shooter's crook.

Boom! Crack!

At the explosive concussion from straight ahead—that very crook he'd noticed—Azzan dropped to a knee, back arched, staring at the heap. The shot muffled his arrival. But if this guy hadn't detected Azzan's approach, then—

Blankets erupted like a volcano. The shooter, rifle tucked against his shoulder, whirled toward Azzan.

Now or never.

He threw himself at the man. The impact carried them into the air. *Oh crap!* Azzan felt the graze of the cement ledge along his leg. Realized the man had been closer to the edge than he'd thought. They were going over. Gravity yanked them down. They fell. Plummeted. He knew better than to brace himself. The impact was going to hurt like a—

Thud!

He hit hard. His teeth clacked. Air punched from his lungs. Groaning on the ground, Azzan told himself to get up. *Move. Breathe.*

Shouts assailed the night.

He felt the man cough beneath him. Shift.

Survival threw Azzan backward. In a fluid move, he snatched out his weapon, cradled and aimed it at the man. His knee buckled, but he held. Saw the man's chest rise . . . raggedly.

Feet pounded behind him.

"He's alive," he called over his shoulder.

Canyon "Midas" Metcalfe dropped next to the man, weapon held down and to the side as he checked his pulse. "Probably not for long after that fall." He glanced up at Azzan. "What about you?"

"Fine."

Midas snorted. "Dude, you're whack. A jump like that." He shook his head, then keyed his mic, calling for a medevac.

It was me or him.

"What about Salih?" Azzan asked about the VIP they'd come to extract.

Midas nodded toward where the guys had been pinned down. "Secure. We'll take him out and call it a success."

"Lygos." Firethorn's voice boomed. "Cut it short, didn't we?"

"*We?*" Azzan turned to the large man. "I didn't see you take the flying leap."

Firethorn came to him, planted a hand on his shoulder, ricocheting aches through Azzan's spine. "That, my friend," he said with a grin, "is because I happen to have what we in the Marines call brains."

"Brains?" Azzan snorted. "My mistake. Thought that was laziness."

Firethorn's guffaw was lost to the *thwump* of approaching rotors.

"Okay, ladies," Actual called, "time to pack it up."

With Salih and the shooter secured, the team made it to the extraction point, another mission successful. Back in Virginia, Azzan showered and changed. He tucked on his wool cap as he stalked to his sport bike, not surprised Max's was already gone. With two kids at home, the guy actually had a life to get back to. In fact, all the guys did now. Griffin's eldest had gone into the Marines to be like his dad, leaving their former spy mom to raise the spitfire, Lyric.

"Hey."

Azzan glanced to where Colton climbed into his oversized black truck.

"Kids were asking about their uncle."

That plied a smile from Azzan.

"Piper expects you for dinner on Sunday."

"Of course." He hadn't missed one in the six years since he'd joined the team. Piper had power-handled the guys on the team. The guys had built lives and families.

And what did he have?

A clear conscience that I haven't put anyone in danger.

"Dude." Canyon slapped his shoulder as he strode past and went for his brand-new red Camaro. "Take care." He tossed his gear into the trunk and opened the driver's door. Then hesitated. Glanced back at Azzan. "You busy tonight?"

Seriously? Canyon had rug rats at home, too. And a beautiful wife.

"I could use your eyes."

Interest sparked, Azzan waited.

"My brother's got this big event coming up in December." Canyon shook his head, which made Azzan wonder. "They're scouting this lodge a couple hours out." He jerked his head to the bay doors. "Come with me. Check it out. Give me your thoughts."

It should bother him that the only time he got invited over was to scout a location.

"I'll buy you a steak dinner."

Azzan smirked. "Done."

"GIRL, THIS PLACE is too Grizzly Adams."

Everly Sinclair laughed. "You've never even seen that show."

"Yeah." Maren Cain rolled her eyes. "And there's a reason— old, out of date, and"—she motioned to the bear's head mounted on the ceiling-to-floor stone fireplace—"bears. Hello!"

Bobbing her head as they crossed the foyer to the information desk, Everly nodded. "I hear you, but this place exudes traditional, conservative values, and that is what our candidate will win on."

"It's two-grand a night per room. How is that conservative?" Maren taunted.

"You know what I mean. We need something to impress those who will carry him to the governor's office next Fall."

"*Assuming* you can pull this off," Harden Frances said as he untied the belt of his trench coat and trailed a disapproving glare over the lodge. "Book something too pricey and our guy looks like he was born with a silver spoon. I told you, education and health-care reform are the way to appeal to—"

Maren smacked the back of his head. "Stand down, overachiever. This is Everly's show."

"No," Everly corrected. "It's *his*." She nodded to the man who entered with an entourage of security and oozing power and authority.

"If I were twenty years older, I would be all over that," Maren said with a click of her tongue.

"Gross, Maren." Though Everly had to admit her friend and team strategist had a point. The man she'd targeted for her first power-play campaign had the looks, the money, and the character.

"What?" Maren said. "He's handsome. Powerful. Good looking. And he's rich—and did I mention gorgeous?"

"Remember 'old'?"

"Ladies, ladies, if you're into powerful and handsome, all you need is right here,"

Ross Nelson said, bowing before them, his black hair flopping into his eyes.

After rolling her eyes at Ross, Everly crossed the grand foyer. "Stone," she said, meeting the man near the fire pit dividing the large gathering space that flung off heavy wooden beams over foyer and lobby. "Thank you for coming out to Bexar-Wolfe Lodge."

Stone Metcalfe clasped her hand, nodding as he took in the luxury setting. "I like it. Cozy but elegant." His blue eyes struck hers. "You don't think it's too much?" He rubbed his jaw, his suit jacket buckling as he moved. "I'm a small-town sheriff—"

"You were. You *were* a small-town sheriff. The Shiraz Case altered that perception," she said, turning toward the front desk, where she spied the lodge's manager and events coordinator she'd met with last week, "and now, I'm going to take that alteration and revolutionize it."

"Hey." He glanced to the doors. "My brother and his buddy are coming up to check this out with me."

Hesitation stalled her brain, stuffing it with defensiveness. Which she shoved down. Way down. "Sure." It was normal he'd want others to check out the lodge as well. Her gaze hit the front entrance, too. "Did you want to wait—"

After checking his watch, Stone shook his head. "Nah. They'll be here and you have a schedule to keep."

"We do." Everly motioned to the events coordinator and led the way to the carpeted conference room.

"Stone," a voice called from behind.

He pivoted and his security detail flanked apart. A younger version of Stone stalked toward them with a grin that matched his brother's. "Canyon. Thanks for coming."

"Anything to show up my big brother."

Annoyed and yet feeling defensive with the new additions, she guided her team into the conference room.

"Whoa," Maren mouthed with a grin, gray eyes wide as she turned to Everly by the oblong table. "Did you see that guy?"

"He's our client's brother," Everly chastised as she drew back the rolling chair.

"No, the other one. Holy moly—runway gorgeous."

"Quiet!" Everly snapped.

"Come on in here," Canyon said. "I want to introduce you."

"I'll be back. Going to look around."

Expecting to see Canyon excusing himself, Everly glanced to the door. Instead, she had to once more admit Maren was right. The "other" guy, the friend. Olive skin. Startling light green eyes. He wore a navy cap that hovered in emphasis over those crazy-pale eyes. His gaze skipped around her friends then paused on Everly. And she'd swear someone had just dumped warm custard over her head!

CHAPTER 2

Northern Virginia

HE EITHER HATED HER or loved her. Azzan pushed past her, Stone, and the other two guys to check out the view from the suite's window. The room was duplicated a hundred times over throughout the lodge, as was the view. The lodge had a pool and courtyard that abutted the base of a nice hill. A steep one dotted with pines and aspens. Thick copse protecting the lodge from brutal snow drifts also created a tight escape route. A line ferried skiers up the hill to the higher elevations for better routes.

A shadow moved and caught his attention in the reflection of the glass. Everly and the hotel guy, Mark, were explaining the room features to Stone.

"Look," Stone said, "as long as the beds are comfortable and clean—"

"We want to make an impression," Everly cut in. "We want them to associate you with taking care of your own. This is the first step."

She shifted, her slacks blending with the dark comforter. Her cream colored blouse stood out as she reached for something on the wall. Light glared against the window, drawing Azzan's attention to the bed lamp. He looked over his shoulder to where Everly stood by the switch.

Her calm demeanor shifted and brought up her chin.

Defensive? Braced?

"What do you think?" Canyon asked quietly, cutting into their line of sight and nodding to the terrain.

Azzan refocused. "Decent." He nodded to the spine of the hill. "Good vantage, but a tough climb. Trees provide cover, but also—"

"Hide problems."

Though he faced out, his mind was inward—on the hazy shadow hovering behind him. She was watching them, listening.

"Lines could be a problem, too," he said, trained on her. "Bring in—"

"It's safe," Everly snipped.

Canyon shifted. Glanced to her, then back to Azzan.

"Okay," Stone said. "Why don't we head to the Brazos and talk about this over steak."

"See?" Canyon slapped his arm. "Promised you a steak."

Azzan snorted. "So why is your brother paying?"

"Think we give security assessments free?" Canyon teased.

They turned, and whether Canyon caught it or not, Azzan sure didn't miss the powerhouse glower from Everly. And a narrowed gaze which seemed to demand who he thought he was to be giving assessments and deciding *her* candidate's venue. In other words, she threw down the gauntlet. Set a challenge before his feet. Would he pick up the glove, respond to her silent command? Or would he walk away?

And that decided it for him.

He loved her.

Confident. Owned the room. Controlled the men. But easily—so very easily—riled. This could be fun.

THE MAN SEEMED intent on ruining plans she'd spent weeks putting into play. Though dinner went well, she had kept her tongue and thoughts to herself while Stone chatted with his brother and the other guy. Who was he? A business partner? What type of business that the Metcalfes so resolutely trusted his advice? Over weeks of research and planning by her team.

Light bloomed and glared from Maren's phone, and her friend bent her head closer with a silent laugh at whatever text she'd received.

Laughter barreled from the guys, who'd managed to seat themselves together, exquisitely excluding Maren and her. She'd grown up in a man's world of politics and maneuvering, but it'd never bothered her. Until tonight.

Because of him. Mr. Green Eyes. With that stubbled jaw and ridiculous beanie—what? Had he forgotten to wash his hair? His dark brows rose in response to something Stone said about his brother and he held a fist to his mouth to hide a laugh.

Everly started at the litter of scars on the back of his hand. And speaking of scars—was that a scar that bisected the lower part of his eyebrow and slid onto his cheekbone. His strong jawline had ridge or two as well. And that shirt of his seemed to struggle to keep the bulge his toned shoulders covered.

"You're staring," Maren muttered, not lifting her head or looking at her.

Everly blinked, only then realizing green eyes were staring back. She stole away her glance and lifted her sweaty water glass. "He's a jerk."

"Why? Because he's gorgeous." Maren laughed, setting down her phone.

"In the hotel, he pointed out every negative thing."

"I think that's his job," Maren said. "Like ours is to point out the positives and keep our guy on track for a solid run."

"But with him making Stone feel unsafe—"

"Hey," someone's gruff voice carried loudly, "weren't you supposed to be talking about the lodge tonight and making some decisions?"

Everly stilled, glancing at Mr. Yasir. That was Middle Eastern, wasn't it? His dark eyes bespoke that heritage, but definitely not the eyes.

"Right." Stone leaned back for the waiter to remove his now-empty plate, and once it was clear, he folded his arms on the table. Nodded at Everly. "I'm impressed, Everly—with the lodge and the research your team has done."

Her heart thudded at the praise. Granddad would be proud. The heady thought pulsed away the annoyance with Azzan Yasir. "Thank you."

Stone smiled. "What date do you have in mind?"

Harden leaned in. "I was thinking—"

"Hey." Azzan Yasir interrupted, pointing to Harden's shirt,

where he'd spilled something. "You're a mess." He stood and passed behind Everly. "I can show you where—"

"I know where the bathroom is," Harden growled.

Seizing the distraction, Everly provided the information. "The team and I thought the week before Christmas."

"Christmas?" Stone frowned. "Nobody wants to be away from their families—"

"Exactly," Everly said with a smirk. "Which is why I negotiated with the lodge to reduce room rates, because the sponsors would be more willing to stay if rates were lowered. I've also negotiated a ski package and a very inexpensive spa package add-on for the wives and daughters."

A genuine smile hit Stone's face. "Nice." He shrugged and motioned to her, Josh, and Maren. "Just let me know what I need to do."

Air swirled, bringing a crisp wintry scent seconds before a presence deposited himself to her right. Body betraying her, Everly fought the uptick in her heart rate. The defiant breath that escaped. If there'd been any doubt who sat beside her, it vanished by the widening of Maren's eyes and pupils.

Everly really did not have time for this. Nor the energy. Her entire career sat at this table in the person of Stone Metcalfe. Nothing was going to ruin this. Not even a pair of wintry green eyes. She shifted to the intruder. "I—" And stopped short.

One, she didn't realize he was that big. Nor his shoulders that broad. Though he seemed lithe and agile before, now he swallowed her visual field. Second, his eyes were closed. Chin tucked to his chest. *Asleep?*

Was she that boring?

"Are you done, Miss?" the waiter asked from her left, extending a hand toward her plate.

With a nod, she leaned aside and let him remove it. Her shoulder bumped Mr. Yasir.

She looked to apologize, and his eyes flashed open.

He swiped a hand over his mouth and straightened in the chair. Met her gaze. "I wasn't arguing with you about the hotel."

Everly stilled, confused. Then her brain caught up with his words and then the meaning. He'd heard her comments to Maren.

And now he was arguing with her about it. She could play dumb or she could own it. He'd called her on this, so the former was out. "I've worked hard to find the right place for Stone to hold his launch event. Next to him, nobody else has more invested in this than me."

Arms folded over his chest, he nodded, gaze roving the restaurant. "It's a good place. Little crowded, but he's right."

Again, more confusion. Why was he saying this? Why couldn't she think past the serene gaze. No, it was intense. Maybe both. And with the lines that scratched at the corners, he had this perpetual smile in his eyes. Like he was laughing. At her?

HER LIPS PARTED in question and Azzan knew he had her. "You did good picking it out."

A flush rose through her cheeks and pulled him closer. Made him angle to face her. Home in on the beauty he'd seen within. The intelligence. The determination.

"What do you do?" she asked.

See? Intelligence. Asking the riskiest of questions. But risk was his crack. "Look for time to kill."

Her eyebrow arched but a smile tugged at her lips. "Not buying it."

With amusement, he hooked his arm over the back of her chair. "Why's that?"

"You don't seem like the type of guy who's lazy and looking to goof off."

"What makes you say that?"

"The way you headed off Harden earlier."

He smirked that she'd noticed. "Did I?"

She smiled—and it made him feel like that moment he'd sailed across rooftops two nights ago. Risk. Thrill. Danger.

But then she veered into uncertainty, and that annoyed him. It didn't look good on her. "I mean—"

"I don't like usurpers."

Surprise smeared away her uncertainty, and in its place came an assuredness, a confidence. "He means well—"

"No, he doesn't."

More surprise.

Some people were inclined to give people the benefit of the doubt. Azzan wasn't. He'd done that before and it nearly cost him his life. "I've met a lot of Hardens in my life. They are out for one thing—themselves. If you doubt someone, there's a reason you doubt them. That can be trusted. Them changing can't."

"That's a pretty jaded view."

"It's realistic."

Chewing her inner cheek, she eyed him. Considered him. And he liked the attention. Wondered what she saw. What she thought. "Don't we all create doubt somehow, let people down because perhaps what we are thinking isn't what they're thinking or expecting?"

A challenge. Directed at him. "Yes." He liked her mind and tell-it-like-it-is-ness. A lot. "But a few do it to the detriment of others."

"Others." A question pinched her eyebrows together. "Who is Harden—"

"You."

Had she stopped breathing? Though this was a typical reaction when he picked a woman, this one felt different. Seemed different. He was pretty sure, even after a short assessment and conversation, that she didn't openly flirt with men. In fact, he could see her toeing the line between being annoyed with his boldness and curiosity about him. Maybe it was a hope she held that he was interested in her.

A claxon sounded in his head. Back off. Give her space. Time to shed that notion.

But he'd never been good at listening to that alarm. In fact, it tended to draw him in. Make his fingers want to brush back the near-black hair curling over her shoulder.

Everly withdrew her gaze and focused on folding the napkin the waiter left.

Should've slowed down. Not that he was interested in a long-term anything. At all. Ever. But this woman seemed worth getting to know.

Her gaze swung to his as if she'd heard his thoughts. "You noticed some apparent weaknesses at the lodge." She wet her lips.

"Uh—security weaknesses." She cleared her throat. Was she seriously that nervous? A little more time and she'd relax, get comfortable talking to him. "Obviously I have a lot of respect for Stone and his family, and they value your opinion"—the mention of his buddy threw his gaze downrange to Canyon and found a glower blasting back—"so I might as well trust you, right?"

Bingo. Just as he'd predicted.

Wait. What? He studied her. What was she saying?

Everly held out her hand. "Your phone."

He frowned. Passed it to her after unlocking it, startled, impressed, concerned that she was going to hand over her number that easily. Not that he'd use it. That fed the fury. The demon within him. Opened doors to his past and the inevitable hope for commitment.

She worked quickly, adding her number to his Contacts. "Whatever thoughts you have on the lodge and added security measures, I'd like to hear them." She returned the phone and came to her feet. As if that had been all business. As if the color rising through her cheeks, inflaming the sprinkle of freckles was nothing unusual.

Addled, Azzan punched out of the seat. Nearly collided with her. Their face inches apart. She startled, stumbling. He caught her waist, which made her go rigid.

She stepped aside. "Good evening, Mr. Yasir." Without looking back, she strode toward Stone, who caught her in a hug as they said good-byes.

Irritation skidded through him at that bit of affection.

"No."

Azzan slid a look to Canyon, who'd come up on his seven.

"No, you're not touching that."

"Excuse me?"

"I know how you dump the girls after a date. Blitz their minds, then kill their hopes."

"Yeah, because you taught me."

Canyon pointed to an exiting Everly. "Off limits."

"Midas—"

"I mean it—she's Stone's ticket to the governor's mansion. Do *not* screw this up for my brother." Canyon's eyes blazed. "Got me?"

"Not a problem."

CHAPTER 3

One Week Later

S ITTING CROSS-LEGGED ON the lush green lawn, Everly stared at the white headstone and wiped away a tear. "I think this is going to work, Grandpa." She hunched against the early-morning chill and leaned her forehead against the cold granite. "And maybe, just maybe, I'll finally do something that will make you proud."

"Be fierce, Evvy. Be fierce."

Recalling his charge to her based off the Shakespeare quote, Everly gritted her teeth. She'd lost so much that night. Not just her grandpa, but any semblance of the "fierce" she possessed then had fallen with those petals. Fisted a hand, remembering the awful night and the assassination. It seemed so pointless. Her grandfather had survived his terms as president, then two years after leaving office, he was killed in their home.

An assassin. A *coward*. Someone not man enough to look her grandfather in the face before ending his life and ripping him away from Everly. He'd been her world.

"I'll do this—you always wanted good men in office, Grandpa." She sniffled and straightened, nodding. "At least I can keep you alive by helping Stone get into the governor's office."

Her phone chimed. Heart skipping a beat in anticipation, she fished it from the pocket of her pink pea coat and glanced at the screen. Her anticipation crashed against the screen and Maren's name. She answered, pushing herself to her feet. "Hey."

"We got him."

Azzan? Everly hesitated. "Who?"

Maren huffed. "Hugh Coton."

Oh. Right. The country singer Stone liked. "Good." She really didn't have a doubt. The guy was an up-and-comer, so a gig at Christmas with a gubernatorial candidate that would pay well . . . Didn't take a genius to know this could impact his career.

She again glanced at the headstone, then brushing off her pants, she started toward her car.

"What's wro—" Maren gasped. "Oh, Ev. I'm sorry. I completely forgot what day—"

"Stop apologizing. It's okay." Had to change gears, distract her friend. But her brain drew a blank. "Look . . ." *Come on, Ev. Think of something.* "I—"

Her phone buzzed. She drew it away from her face and checked the screen, which made her heart flip. The unknown number not so much. But . . . the message.

Up security measures at rear of facility and tree line. Ask for help to cover paths and lifts. Extra manpower during big gatherings. Secure Metcalfe's room and verify his detail are legit. Hire a security consultant.

Nerves trilling—he'd texted her!!—Everly made her way through the sea of headstones onto a sidewalk. The message wasn't signed. But it was obvious who'd sent it.

A distant voice reminded her Maren was on the line still. "Helllooo? Where'd you go?"

"Yeah. I'm here. Listen, I think"—she eyed the headstone one more time—"we need to up security." She then relayed the details Azzan provided.

"Wait. He called?"

"Gotta go, Maren." After ending the call, she climbed into her car and started the engine. She read his text again. And again. Thrilled—stupidly, but . . . No. *"How are you? Want to grab coffee?"* Business. He was all business.

Except, he wasn't. She'd seen it in his eyes. Should she invite him to work with her on this? His confidence bled into arrogance that both annoyed and impressed her.

Does this mean you're available?

Her thumbs hovered over the keyboard. Chewing her lower lip, she realized asking him to do this was more forward than was normal for her, but maybe . . . maybe that part of her hadn't died with Grandpa.

Everly hit send and dropped her phone in the console before she could change her mind. She signaled to pull into traffic and glanced over her shoulder, waiting for an opening. Her phone chimed, sending her pulse overboard. She grabbed it.

Not looking for a relationship.

"What . . .?" *Available.* Oh no! Not what she meant. *Sorry. I meant the job.*

Relax, Beautiful. Canyon already wrangled me into this. I'll be there.

Thanksgiving

"UNCLE AZZAN!" A blond ball of energy launched at him as he crossed the threshold. With split-second reaction, he caught the blur in his arms. Tossed her up and over his back, eliciting a squeal from three-year-old Sophia. Her hair hit his face as he hooked a hand and secured her on his shoulders.

Her older brother, Ben, slid around the corner, boots skidding on the wood floor as he aimed a toy rifle at him. Fired a foam bullet. It hit Azzan's leg.

With a groan and clutching his thigh, Azzan went down on a knee. "This is Three. I'm down. Digitalis, send evac."

Delight gleamed in the boy's eyes.

"Daddy," Sophia called, long and loud, "Ben's shooting inside again!"

"Am not!" The boy struck a defiant pose, but held onto his weapon.

He was a natural. Made Azzan proud.

"Ben," Colton's remonstrative tone came from the back of the house just before the thud of his boots. He entered the living room, carrying a rambling smaller version of himself—and Sophie's twin—complete with a plaid shirt, jeans, and boots. The bigger cowboy met his gaze but never hesitated. "Azzan. Didn't know you were here."

He clasped hands with his cousin's husband. "Sophie let me in," he said, lowering the little girl to the floor.

"Oh, good," Piper said as she peeked out of the kitchen. "Just in time."

Colton clicked his tongue. "Sounds like she's putting us to work again."

"Should I make a run for it?" A buzzing in his back pocket had Azzan pulling out his phone.

"Don't even try." Piper grinned as she kissed his cheek, then started to the kitchen.

While Sophia grabbed his finger and Ben fired another foam round, Azzan read the screen.

Her: *Thanksgiving and big family dinners. *Who* thought this was a good idea?*

He snorted. They had a lot in common. He loved his nieces, but they came in small doses that he could handle. More people than Colton, his mom, and Piper, and Azzan would probably dig up decent excuses.

Him: *No joke. as bad as vetting political events with people I don't know.*

Her: *You can be a coward and back out.*

Him: *Really?*

Her: *Nope.*

He grinned at the response. At her strength.

"What is that?"

Azzan glanced up to find Piper standing in front of him, hands on her hips, offense in the familial green eyes they'd inherited from their grandmother. "What?"

"That." She pointed to his phone.

"It's a—"

"I know *what* it is!" Piper growled.

"Then why'd you ask?" It was too easy to distract and rile his cousin.

Piper huffed at him. "*Why* do you have one? You said you'd never own one. When'd you get it?"

He stared at her blankly, stunned, thinking back to Everly's text about family and gatherings. Thinking hard to explain why he was texting anyone, let alone a beautiful young woman. "Which question am I supposed to answer first?"

"Answering a question with a question is a sign of guilt, Azzan Yasir." She snapped her head toward the device. "You said you didn't have one."

"I didn't."

"But you do."

He held it up.

"Don't you get smart with me." Her eyes narrowed to razor slits and warning. "I could've been calling you. Why didn't you tell me?"

He snorted. "What? And get put to work?"

Annoyance creased her features. "You won't give your number to your last remaining relative, but you'll give it to"—she peered at it again but he tucked it into his back pocket, along with his embarrassment over Everly—"Who was that?"

"Nobody. Work."

"Work." She arched an eyebrow. "Normally, you're a very good liar."

Azzan looked at Colton, pleading with him to call off his wife, but the cowboy lifted his hands and headed out the side door with a trail of kids in his wake. "Coward," he called after him.

"Work does not make you smile like that," Piper noted.

That was the beauty of this situation. "It really does." He started for the kitchen. "Hello, Mrs. Neeley. How are you?"

Later that night as he lay on the queen bed in the guest room, he reached for the phone. Paused. Surprising himself that he had so quickly become addicted to talking to her. Surprised at how much he wanted to hear her voice, which he could with each text, even though she didn't speak. She was in those words. And in that, she was with him.

Him: *Did you survive? In turkey coma now?*

She was with family, so there wouldn't be a reply any time—

His phone dinged.

Her: *I wish! Parents are arguing as always. Wish Grandpa was here.*

Him: *That bad?*

Her: *Worse. Grandpa always knew how to steal the show from their antics. He always made me laugh.*

Him: *Not sure what's worse—no family or bad family.*

Her: *Trust me on this one: bad family. In a way, I've got both now.*

His thumbs twitched to tell her his tale. But . . . it was too much. Or was it? He considered her words. Considered her openness with him.

Him: *I had no family until my cousin married. Good in small doses.*

Her: *Glad to know you're not alone tonight.*

Azzan couldn't bring himself to reply. Couldn't bring himself to ask about her. He wanted to. He wanted to tell her they should meet. Maybe he could make her laugh again. But that'd be crossing too many lines. Wasn't there a jinx about that?

"HI, THIS IS EVERLY SINCLAIR. I'm calling to verify that you have everything necessary for the filing and declaration of Stone Metcalfe as gubernatorial candidate."

"Everly! It's me—Deena Mikals. How are your parents doing?"

Taken aback at the familiar voice, Everly lost her train of thought. Her parents? "They're good." Vacationing in the Caribbean. They'd never been close, more a facilitated family arrangement than a marriage. Something she sure didn't want.

"Oh, Everly, looks like you still need to get some documents in."

"What?" She sucked a breath and nearly choked. "I . . . my staff said they were there."

"Well, we have a pretty rigorous process of recording when the pieces come in and when they're approved. I see two missing documents. If you'll give me a second to pull that up . . ."

Even as Everly wrote down the particulars, she realized an ugly truth. They were both assigned to Harden. She sat forward at her desk, buzzing with shock. "I'm sorry—they'll be on your desk tonight."

"Good, because tomorrow's the deadline to turn it in."

This time, she couldn't trust anyone else to be responsible for this. "Thanks, Deena."

"No problem, Everly. But you know, honestly? I'd expected more from your team than disorganization like this," Deena said.

"I couldn't agree more."

"Well, tell your parents hello for me."

"Will do. Bye." She shoved her fingers along her scalp and fisted her hair with a stifled groan.

"That doesn't look good," Maren said, dropping into the chair at her desk.

"I called to verify everything had been filed and we were good to go, only to discover the two I assigned Harden are missing."

"Um, F for teamwork." Maren huffed. "I have no idea why you wanted him on the campaign—"

"Because if he funneled that effort into the campaign, instead of one-upping me, he'd be an asset."

"Yeah, except now, it's just the first part of that word."

Everly tried to stifle her laugh, but failed. "I've printed them off and need to get them out there today."

"I'm headed that way. I can take them."

When Everly hesitated, Maren rolled her eyes. "Unlike Harden, I want this for you as much as I want it for Stone. I'll get it done. Besides, you have enough troubles."

"Like?"

"Harden. It's officially December. Event's in twenty days. Snow's in the forecast."

Seriously, the world was against her. But maybe not. She had to be positive, right? "It can snow—just not much and not on the night of the event."

Maren saluted, her dark bangs ruffling over her eyes. "I'll give the weather your orders." Her friend leaned over and gently slapped Everly's leg. "Hey, cheer up. All in all, this campaign is going very well."

"It helps having a strong, likeable candidate."

"Fielded a question earlier from a reporter over rumors you're dating him."

"Who?" Everly recoiled. "Stone?" She snorted. "He's too old for me. Besides, that'd be like dating an older brother. Gross." Lifting a report from the corner of her desk, she saw her phone's screen brighten. So did her mood.

"The caterer asked again for a final count."

"Told them"—she picked up her phone—"that won't happen until next week."

Him: Walked the site. Recruited operators. Ninety percent readiness.

Her: Only 90? Falling down on the job, huh?

Him: Only if you make me put skis on.

Her: What? You can't ski?

Him: You can?

Her: Junior Olympian here.

Him: Guess you'll have to teach me.

Everly laughed. That could be—

"Okay, I can't take it anymore!" Maren stomped to her feet, then snatched the phone away from Everly. "I have to know what you two are texting."

"Hey!" Everly's heart stuttered at the thought of her friend reading those messages. "He's talking about the security measures for—"

"He's *flirting* with you." Maren gaped, craning her neck forward. "And you're doing it back."

"No." Cheeks aflame, she shrugged. "Maybe a little."

"You don't even know him!"

"You're the one always telling me I'm too wrapped up in my

career and the campaign," Everly said, retrieving her phone. "That I need to breathe and date."

"I know, but," Maren said with a sigh, "not when you're working your first major campaign! He's your security consultant. What if you're all hot and heavy that night and he misses something—"

"I will not be hot and heavy!" She laughed, but the words were a good smack to her common sense. She took a step back and a long breath. "But . . . you're right." She couldn't afford a misstep or distraction. Even over wintry green eyes. She met her friend's sympathetic gaze. "Thank you."

"Look," Maren said, sitting on the edge of the desk, "don't run him off. He's gorgeous. And if he likes you, then he might be just what you need—*after* the campaign. A nice New Year's Eve with Green Eyes. Just . . . tell him you can't do this now. If he sticks around, he's legit. If not, then you're better off without him."

Why did that thought spear her? She hadn't even been thinking long-term. Just . . . now. The way his texts made her smile. The way he was always there. Which was weird because he wasn't. He was texting. He could be in Japan for all she knew.

"I'm going to head out and beat rush hour, so I can get these to court on time."

"Thanks," Everly said, watching her friend and partner leave the rented office. When she heard the thud of the door, she dropped back against her chair with a huff. Rubbed her temple. How could she be so foolish to entertain anything with Azzan? She knew nothing about him and she was drowning trying to get this campaign up and running. Once the candidacy was announced, things would get really crazy.

It was probably her distraction with him that allowed her to miss Harden's sleight of hand, trying to usurp power.

Yet, was she never to find someone? Was she to be alone all her life? Because this was her career path. This—campaigning—would be her future. She wasn't going to walk away just because of some guy.

Her phone lit, and again, took her heart. She ignored it. Had to. Stay focused, right?

She rubbed her hands over her face then glanced around her

desk for something to plant her attention on.

The phone vibrated.

She gritted her teeth. Turned to the dusty windows.

Vibrated again.

She closed her eyes.

Again.

Huffing, she snatched the phone up. Read, but don't reply. She could to that.

Him: *You okay?*

A few seconds another one: *Does the thought of me skiing scare you that much?*

And then: *Okay. No skiing. Probably safest since I'll be armed.*

Last: *Will you be armed? That'll imprint on your slinky dress. Just saying. I won't mind though.*

Gaping at his boldness, she scoffed.

Her: *What makes you think I'll be wearing something like that?*

Him: *Because you're gorgeous and deserve it.*

Her: *Isn't that sexist?*

Him: *I think you meant to type SEXY.*

She sniffed a laugh. Shook her head at his playfulness, his audacity. He was probably way more trouble than she should be near, but it was nice—he was nice. Her phone buzzed.

Him: *Seriously. No offense. Just wanted to see you smile again.*

Wanted to see you smile . . .

Could he see her? Everly snapped up her head, then slowly pushed her gaze to the windows. He didn't mean that literally, did he? Maybe he meant *make* her smile again. Not *see* her smile again.

Her: *Can you see me?*

Him: *Do you want me to?*

What did that mean? Wait—was he reading into her words again, thinking she was asking him out? Maren's warning sailed against her surprisingly strong hope that he was misunderstanding. That he'd ask her out.

Her: *Got to get back to work. See you on the 20th.*

Him: *How about a test? If you *can* see me, you don't have to pay me.*

Did he mean on the night the event started? Or did he mean now? She laughed, but felt a nervous, almost giddy unease. Her gaze again drifted to the windows. *Was* he out there? The building across the street was one-story and empty. No cars. No other windows. So, he couldn't be out there.

Her: *Deal.*

December 10ᵗʰ

AZZAN RAN, TRACING the foot-wide ledge of the wall, pitched himself off it . . . landing with a soft thump on the large, yellow foam pad. He rolled through it then jogged across the warehouse empty of anything save the rudimentary parkour equipment. He dropped and did a dozen push-ups, then hopped to his feet again. After a hundred reps, Azzan slapped the three-foot-high wall with his palms and hoisted himself over to the other side. Back and forth. Back. Forth.

Then he took a running start at the brick wall. Nailed it with the balls of his feet and shoved to the left. Caught the bar and swung himself up, and back . . . then up and over. Bar pressed into his pelvic bones, he steadied himself for a second, then rolled back over, released. And dropped with a soft thump onto the ground. He was off, running again at a cement wall. He jumped at it and caught the ledge. Pulling himself up. He ran its spine, then pitched himself off the ledge. Sailing through the air. Landing with a soft thump on a large foam pad. He rolled through it and came up, jogging toward a curved wall. He scurried up it and gripped its ledge, then twisted and slid back down.

Breathing heavy, he hooked his forearms on his knees and stared at the gray mat. She hadn't texted since that last message. He hadn't misread her, but he'd expected more dialogue. He wanted more dialogue.

Which would go over real well with Midas.

Insane. Was it because of Midas's warning that Azzan violated his own rules, violated his promise to steer clear of relationships? Piper had been right—he never owned a phone. Now, he felt tied to it. Vainly hoping she'd text him. Loving it when she did. Hating it when she didn't.

Shoving to his feet, he grabbed the nearby cloth and wiped it over his face.

But man, it'd been good to see that smile back on her face. He'd slipped into the building without anyone noticing, keeping his skills brushed up, but what he saw and heard, stopped him. He wasn't sure what her friend said to her, but watching that smile, the joy ebb from her fair complexion, bugged him.

Which was stupid. She was not going to give him the time of day. At least not for long. No woman would. Not once they knew what he had been, what he was. Work black ops wasn't much different.

His phone rattled across the mat. He picked it up, glad for the text. Angry, too.

Her: Market Square two hours ago.

He smirked at her bad guesses and the obvious hope in her texts about whether he'd been at the same location she'd visited.

Him: Negative.

Her: You know it's cheating to stay home and never go anywhere, so you can claim I never saw you.

Him: Blue sweater. Paisley flats. Bow earrings.

Her: Is that your shopping list?

Him: What you were wearing the last time I saw you.

Her: Liar. That's what I have on now.

Him: I should double my fee.

Her: That's blackmail.

Him: Triple?

Her: Or I could fire you for being such a bad liar.

December 12ᵗʰ

SUN BEAT IN through the windshield, thrusting a piercing glare into Everly's eyes as she parked in front of the coffee shop. She groaned and peered up through puffy clouds. "Let drop your dew," she pleaded, "in the form of frozen flakes."

A snow-less week in the mountains at the lodge wouldn't exactly ruin the week, but it wouldn't exactly help either.

And she needed help. With Harden's antics and the sudden rise of another possible candidate in the form of Senator Craig Ballister . . .

Turning off her engine, she looked at the signage that was a coffee cup with steam spiraling up. "I so need you." She grabbed her phone and climbed out, hustling toward the door.

Her phone dinged, signaling a text.

Excited, she glanced at her phone.

"Excuse me," a man said, cutting her off and opening the door.

She grunted. "Rude." But the unexpected but very wanted text threw a crooked smile onto her lips as she scurried into the shop behind the man.

Him: One week. Ninety five percent readiness.

She smiled as she inched forward toward the register.

Maren said to steer clear of Azzan. Focus on the campaign.

Right. She left the text and opened email. Replied to an email she'd put off. Crafted a memo for the team, complete with a list—"

"Hey, Ev. Usual?"

Everly smiled at the barista. "Please—extra shot today, Keira."

"You got it." The barista plucked a red cup from the pile, scratched on it with a black marker, and as she set the cup in the line, she rang it up. "You're good to go."

"Don't I need to pay for it?" Everly said with a laugh, hoisting her phone up so the scanner could catch the app.

"Nope. It was paid ahead."

Everly stilled. "Really?" She blinked. She'd heard of people doing that, but never had it happen to her.

"Hey, Keira," someone called from the back.

The barista waved to Everly and started toward the office and supply area.

Everly scooted along, wondering who'd paid for her. Surely not the rude guy—which, speaking of . . . where'd he go? She glanced around the restaurant. Scanned the twenty-, thirty-, forty-somethings working on laptops and holding meetings. Looked like there was even an interview happening in the corner.

Her phone chimed and she glanced at it, then scowled at the preview of the email that had hit her inbox. She opened it. Read. "No no no." She gritted her teeth. "Harden, you were the biggest mistake . . ." He'd gone behind her back again.

"Everly!" a barista on bar called, setting her drink on the serving ledge.

"Thanks," Everly said, stepping forward. Even as her fingers skimmed the edge, she saw the words written there. *Seen me yet?* And froze.

Her breath jammed into her throat.

"Don't turn around." His breath rushed along the nape of her neck and sent chills. She flinched, her fingers grazing the cup and sending it over the ledge. "No!" Everly yelped and lunged at the cup. It wobbled but dropped into her hand. Sloshing searing-hot coffee over the ridge of her thumb and the soft, fleshy part. She growled through her clumsiness but couldn't shake the blackened vision that rushed through her—instead of coffee, she saw pale pink petals. Instead of the bar, she saw marble and iron.

She righted her cup. Shook out her hand, head spinning. She jerked around to give him a piece of her mind. But she found nobody there.

Nobody.

How was that possible?

Hand stinging, she turned a circle. Looked to the baristas, who were worrying over her burn. Keira rushed at her with a burn gel packet and bandage. "Oh my gosh! Are you okay?"

"Where is he?" Everly demanded.

"Who?"

"The man who wrote on my cup. The one who was behind me and made me spill."

"Ev, I wrote on your cup."

"*You* wrote that?" Everly asked, pointing to the words.

Keira paused, then frowned. "Uh, no." She scrunched up her brow. "I have no idea how that got there."

"He was there. Right there—behind me. Said not to look." She touched her nape, an inch of skin bare above her scarf. "I felt his breath . . ."

Keira arched her eyebrow.

What if it wasn't him, but the . . . killer? The one who'd stolen her grandpa from her? "I . . . I need to go." She took the cover, rejecting the cream and bandage. She rushed out, furtively glancing around as she hurried to her car.

An envelope sat beneath the windshield wiper. "Marketers," she growled and snatched it. In her car, she dropped the cup in the holder, groaned when it sloshed again. Tears pricked her eyes. She tossed aside the envelope and a spray of pink fluttered free.

Everly hauled in a breath, staring in disbelief at the petals that drifted to the floorboard.

She swallowed, the memory flinging her back several years. The night Grandpa died. She closed her eyes, remembering how the nape of her neck had felt chilled. The assassin had slipped into the house, killed him, knocked her into a dark abyss before vanishing again into the night.

She shook her head. "Though he's killing my every hope of staying focused, Azzan's not an assassin." But if not him, who had left the envelope?

December 17

IT'D BEEN A MISTAKE to spook her like that. He hadn't meant to scare her. It'd wrecked him to watch her sit in the car and cry. He'd caused that. And it gutted him. It was a lesson. A reminder. That'd be her reaction when she learned the truth about him.

Azzan ran a hand over his face. Stared at the phone. The text he had typed two days ago. The one he couldn't send.

He'd broken his own rules communicating with her. He knew better. He was the Barret MRAD sniper rifle. She the delicate bloom destroyed by crossing his path. If he was honest with himself, he'd already crossed the line with Everly. She had this way about her that made him want to be there. Made him want to make her smile. Keep it there. Whatever it took. It looked good on her. Made her glow. That black-as-night hair. Those gold eyes. Porcelain skin. That smile. He'd probably pay money to see it because it did something weird to him. Made him feel drunk. Made him get careless. Do stupid things.

And that was exactly how he'd get her killed. Lose situational awareness.

He stood and flung the phone across the room. It struck the wall and shattered, pieces shearing off and raining on the wood floor.

Hands on his head, Azzan stood and paced. Gritted his teeth. He wouldn't. He'd gotten soft with Raiyah, and her brother shot her in the head.

Not doing that again. Wouldn't cost another girl her life. Or anyone, unless they were deliberately on the business-end of his weapon. Everly wasn't a mission. Stone wasn't a mission. There was no danger like what he faced with Nightshade.

So, there wasn't any danger. She'd stay alive.

Especially if he stayed *away*.

He moved to the window and folded his arms over his chest, hands tucked up into his armpits. He heard the boards creak near his door. Glanced over his shoulder. Colton eyed the shattered remains on the floor. Dragged a speculative look to Azzan. "You okay?"

He gave a slight nod. "Phone fell."

"From what cliff?"

CHAPTER 4

December 21

AIMING HER SILVER CROSSOVER through the lightly drifting snow and up the winding road shot adrenaline through Everly's veins—along with a hefty injection of anxiety. He hadn't messaged her or called since the moment at Starbucks. She pulled into to a spot closest to the front entrance and slid the shifter into PARK. Hugging her steering wheel, Everly stared at the front of the lodge, bedecked in Christmas wreaths with glistening ribbon trickling around its curves. Lights traced the door frame. Through the sidelights, she could see the warm glow of a fire and the twenty-foot Christmas tree, glittering with myriad colored lights.

The brightness of the lights made her more aware of the day's gray pallor and darkening sky. She lifted her eyes to the clouds, and craning her neck a little farther, considered the falling snow. "Just give me the next few days," she whispered to the elements, then thought better. "Lord, please—let this go off well."

Thump!

With a yelp, Everly jumped back, heart racing as she stared at the clump of snow that had hit her windshield. Where had that—

Movement at the door caught her attention. Maren bent over, gathering a white ball into her hands. With a laugh, Everly honked the horn and then pushed open her door. "No fair," she taunted. "You don't want to see me in a snowball fight. My grandfather taught me some mean skills in launching those." Another one came sailing over the car door, and she ducked. Then straightened and glowered at her friend. "Aren't you supposed to be doing something—like helping me bring in all this stuff?" She pointed to her trunk.

"And who helped me with mine?" Maren asked as she came around the back of the vehicle. "Actually, the really cute facilities guy helped me."

Everly rolled her eyes, glancing at the door. "Any sign of—"

"Thought you were putting that romance thing off until after this?"

"—Harden or Ross." She huffed.

"Neither of them are here yet."

With a frown, Everly glanced at her phone to check the time.

"Hey, I'm not doing all the work," Maren grumbled as she lifted a plastic tub from the back of the crossover.

Lifting two more bins out, she was glad her friend had brought up Azzan, answering the question begging to be voiced. He wasn't here either. But he would be. Eventually. At least, he should be. She wasn't sure what happened, why he'd gone silent. She just hoped he showed up for this event. With the sponsors and backers heading this way with their families for a pre-Christmas event and mini-vacation, she needed the assurance that security was handled.

Conveniently, like a blister, Ross and Harden showed up once all the unloading had been handled. After a meeting with the lodge owner and event coordinator, they were holed up in a conference room, where they worked preparing loot bags, welcome packets, and making last-minute calls to the caterers—one for the food, one for the flowers, and one for the gift baskets that would be placed in the each of the rooms. Thankfully, the lodge had an indoor playground and the children onsite would be attended by additional staff Everly had hired—childcare workers from her church's center, which was closed for the week. This event would be extravagant, but that was the point, showing that Stone Metcalfe was here to stay, until he took the governor's mansion.

When deep, rumbling voices carried down the hall outside the conference room, Everly felt her pulse skip a few beats. She glanced at Maren. "Sounds like Stone is here." She set down a folder and pushed back her chair. Even as she turned, she saw three large frames fill the doorway.

She met Stone's gaze and gave him a smile. "You ready?"

He drew in a breath, pulling his shoulders up, glanced at his brother and another man with a cowboy hat in hand, then let it out.

"As ready as I'll ever be." With a nod, he met Harden's gaze. "Thanks for sending over that itinerary. Nice work, by the way."

Heat swarmed Everly's neck and shoulders. "Itinerary?"

"Yeah," Stone said, swiping a finger over his mouth. "For the week."

Oh. The one *she* had created? The one *she* had sent to the team? The one *she* sent to the hotel? The one she had failed to CC Stone on. Harden had noticed her slip and seized the chance to make himself look good. Again.

But calling him on it would only make her look bad and point out the mistake of not having sent it to Stone herself. Which she should have done. So she had to regain control.

"Have you checked in?" she asked, moving closer to them.

"We have," he said, nodding to the others.

She hesitated on the cowboy, unsure if she should know him.

He stretched out a large hand. "Colton Neeley, ma'am."

Ah. She recalled his name on the guest list with a wife and four children. "Everly Sinclair," she said, accepting his greeting. "I'm . . ." She looked at Stone, letting the frown of question flicker through her face.

"Colton's here because Azzan brought him," Canyon said.

Azzan. "Oh." Everly nodded. "Security." So where was this so-great security officer?

Colton nodded. "He around?"

"Afraid not," she said, reaching for her leather binder and turning back to her candidate. "If you're ready, we can do a walkthrough of the facilities and how tomorrow evening's welcome dinner will go."

Stone rubbed his hands together. "Let's get this started."

He really was a handsome man, with his blonde hair and blue eyes, broad shoulders, and a weathered look that said he'd been there, done that. Even now in his leather jacket and a dangling scarf, he still exuded the "I'm in charge" attitude that came with a dozen years in law enforcement. She really hoped he found someone because that was a lot of good man going to waste.

The ballroom was already taking shape with the tables set up and chairs gathered. The "New Sheriff in Town" banner swayed as the event decorators worked to get it steadied. Balloons and drapes would be hung behind the podium that stood at the far right of the room.

They went over the schedule for the evening, which she handed to him from the folder. Thankfully, she'd gotten a little behind and hadn't emailed that one out.

"Since I'm helping with security," Colton said, "wouldn't it be smart to have me at the back of the room?"

"I believe"—*where is Azzan?*—"there are hired security officers from the hotel, who will serve that function."

"Miss Sinclair?"

Everly turned toward the door.

The lodge manager, Ephraim Daily, was jogging toward her. "I think we have a problem."

She tensed. "What kind?"

"Security." He nodded to the back wall. "We had that security installed that you requested, and it just got tripped."

Frowning, she glanced to Stone and Colton.

"Skiers?" Canyon asked, shouldering into the conversation.

"Lifts are closed," Mr. Daily said, "as is the whole lodge, until after Christmas for this event. Nobody should be out there."

"But it's too soon for an attack, isn't it?" Harden said with a laugh.

"Never known trouble too early," Colton said.

Canyon slapped his friend's shoulder as he swept past. "Let's check it out."

A wave of dread swept through Everly. This could not be happening already.

CHAPTER 5

CROUCHED ON A tree limb, Azzan stared through the limbs to the side entrance of the lodge. Pleased that they'd detected his movement, though he'd been obvious enough. But he had to admit, the greatest pleasure was seeing the raven-haired woman step out into the thin blanket of snow.

Two security guards moved into the open, swiping back their suit jackets, the power play for their weapons obvious. And cheesy. They would've been dead already if that's what he'd wanted.

Amusement teased the edges of his nerves as the suits stalked forward.

Cowboy lifted his chin, saying something—obviously telling them to stay back because the suits then returned to their charge. Stone. Man, these guys needed some serious lessons from Nightshade. Speaking of . . . two more and the team would be reassembled. That was when his misgivings about this location would be eased. A fraction.

Everly ran one hand along her nape and the other hugged her waist. Probably remembering when he'd spooked her. And was he doing it again now? Why was she so skittish? It didn't seem like her.

When Canyon shifted to go back inside. Azzan dropped the ten feet from the branch with a soft thump, the snow padding the noise. Eyes never leaving the group, he saw Canyon find him first. Then Everly. Then her security, who snapped weapons up.

"Easy," Cowboy growled to the guards. "He's ours."

"Was that necessary?" Canyon asked as Azzan made his way to them.

"Testing the systems," he muttered.

Canyon smirked. Gripped his forearm. "Kind of obvious,

weren't you?"

"That why you nearly went back inside?"

With his crooked smile, Canyon considered him. Then shrugged. "I was bored."

"Right." Ducking, Azzan stole a glance at Everly—and collided with a pair of gold eyes that locked and loaded before he could withdraw. That instant telegraphed her still-evident attraction, her hurt, her confusion. That was the 'loaded'—packing his shoulders with the guilt of not returning her messages.

Canyon slapped his back. Hard.

A warning.

As the others filed back inside, Azzan hung back to put distance between him and Everly. He had to admit—being around her made him feel as if someone had set a bomb. If he tried to deactivate it, the thing would blow. Yet, with enough time, it'd blow.

In a small conference room with more chairs and less air, Azzan planted his back to the wall nearest the door. Watched the others review final details with Everly and her team.

An arm snaked around the door, reaching for him.

Instinct reared. He grabbed the wrist. Stepped out and around. Yanked the person into the jamb.

Oof!

Griffin side stepped, laughing, holding his shoulder, which had taken the brunt of the impact.

Max came in behind him, laughing. "Man, you are so predictable, Aladdin."

"Good. Glad you're all here," Stone said as he rounded the table and shook their hands. "Good to see you again. Have you checked in?"

Max and Griffin nodded.

"Perfect," Stone said, turning to Everly. "Just in time for dinner, right?"

She brushed a long bang from her face as she straightened. "Yes. Dinner's in the lodge restaurant, so you could all make your way over there now."

Why wasn't she coming?

Stone, his security detail and the Nightshade team started out of the room. Though Azzan knew he should go, too, he somehow hadn't left the conference area yet.

After tucking a pen in her mouth, Everly lifted several files into her arms. She deposited them in a box, then swung around for more—and stopped short, looking at him. Hands on her small waist, she drew up her shoulders. "So, I guess we failed your security check."

"They're not as good as my team," he admitted. "But the guys are here now."

She blew that length of hair from her face and gave him a wary glance. "Well, I guess that's something."

Annoyed. It should be expected, but it still struck him wrong.

"If you'll excuse me, Maren and Ross and I need to get this stuff boxed up and locked away for the night."

"How can I help?"

She nodded to the door. "Shut the door on your way out."

Surprise shoved his eyebrows up. He'd really ticked her off, hadn't he? Though he watched her, noted the color creeping beneath those freckles that lined her nose and cheeks of her fair skin, he also noted the way the others shot her a glance. As surprised as him. "Understood." Azzan stalked out of the room and shut the door.

And there in the hall, he flinched when he saw the guy standing at the hall juncture between the offices and the grand foyer. Canyon.

"What'd I say?" Canyon growled.

Azzan lifted his hands. "She put me in charge of security. I'm doing my job."

"That's all it better be," Canyon said. "My brother's been through a lot. He deserves this. Don't want that messed up."

"He's the brother of a friend," Azzan agreed as he started past his buddy. "I don't want to see it messed up either, no matter what I think about politicians."

"Hey," Canyon said, breaking into a broad grin as he looked past Azzan.

With a boy in her arms and pre-teen girl holding her hand, Dani Metcalfe descended the stairs and glided across the floor to Canyon. He kissed her, then took the boy from her. After a nod to Azzan, they headed to the lodge restaurant.

Laughter spiraled from a side hall and there emerged Colton with Piper, who passed a writhing Spencer over to his father. Eleven-year-old McKenna had her sedate sister, Sophia, propped on her hip. The twins had been a surprise to Colton and Piper, but they were the kind of people who deserved big families. They knew how to do 'family' right. Unlike Azzan.

Little Ben's face brightened. "Uncle Azzan!" Boots clomping, the five-year-old ran—well, trudged because of his boots—over to him.

Hefting the boy up, Azzan savored what he could of family life. "Hey, how's my partner?" He swung the solid guy up onto his shoulders.

"Reporting for duty, sir," Ben said, probably snapping a salute as he always did.

"You coming?" Piper asked, nodding toward the long hall that led to the restaurant.

His mind skipped back to the door he'd just closed. "Lead the way."

A buffet afforded Stone's staff and the Nightshade team a nice selection of foods. Azzan stuck to the vegetables and chicken, finishing off quickly, knowing the twins would get restless. And it was a good way for him to extricate himself as conversations turned toward socializing. With every other Nightshade member married and producing offspring, the talk invariably came back to Azzan and his dating life. His nonexistent dating life. Sure, he'd met a girl or two at a bar. Went to a movie. Never more than once. Enough to say he'd done it. Enough to realize the risks were too high.

Invariably, his gaze drifted down range to the woman seated by Stone and his mother, who'd joined them for the dinner. Everly's laughter billowed out at something Mrs. Metcalfe said.

Canyon lifted a hand to the doorway, where his younger siblings, Range and Willow appeared. The winsome beauty kissed Dani on the cheek, then dropped into the seat beside Azzan. She bumped his shoulder.

"You look bored already, Aladdin."

"That would be because I am," he grinned. Willow was a beauty alright, and they'd done the one-date thing, both deciding it was too much like dating a sibling. They settled on a firm, comfortable friendship.

"Have they asked if you're dating yet?" Willow asked, reaching for a biscuit.

"Not yet." He folded his arms on the table, watching her spread jam on the biscuit. "But now that you sat here and smiled at me, they'll assume we're engaged."

"Oh, when are we getting married?" She scooped butter onto the biscuit.

"Spring's probably best."

"So soon?"

"If we're in love, no time to waste."

She bit into the biscuit with a grunt-nod. "Definitely," she said around the crumbs. She brushed her long, thin blond hair from her face, then wagged her fingers at him. "I need a ring. An expensive one."

"I thought you shunned material things?"

"Not when it comes to a lifetime commitment."

Azzan laughed. He felt a tug at his sleeve and glanced behind him, not surprised to find little Sophia. "Hey, princess." He lifted her up, nudging aside the plates and setting her on the edge of the table.

AN ACHE BLOOMED in her chest as she watched Azzan with the pretty blonde—both the grown up one and the child he teased and whose neck he nuzzled his jaw against, eliciting peals of laughter from her. It was beautiful, the way he was with the children. Not so much as he was with the woman.

Everly couldn't decide if the ache was from her deep desire for a family, or if it was jealousy digging its claws into her heart. Maybe both. It sure didn't help that Maren devoted so much of her energy to flirting with Stone's youngest brother. Granted, Range Metcalfe was very similar to his older brother but had none of the swagger of his next-oldest. In fact, he seemed an uncertain middle between Stone's quiet, solid disposition and Canyon's confident, near-arrogant personality. And of course, Harden was down there flirting with the leggy blond, too.

"Anyone heard from Brooke?" Stone asked.

"Her flight got delayed in London," Canyon said. "She said she might not make it."

"Convenient," Range muttered.

Canyon scowled at him.

"It's true. She agrees to each family event, then miraculously misses every one."

"This is neither the time nor the place to air laundry, Range," Mrs. Metcalfe said, then touched Everly's arm. "I'm so impressed with what you've lined up for the next few days."

"Thank you," Everly said, glancing at Stone who smiled. "I know it's a packed schedule for Stone, but I was able to pull some strings and get more lined up than I'd anticipated. That speaks to the candidate's reputation." She gave another nod to her client.

"That speaks to each person's need for a part in the game," Stone countered.

"Don't be so morose! You're a good man, and they know it," Mrs. Metcalfe said. "Of course they want to partner with success."

"You're my mom." Stone laughed. "You have to say that."

Laughter barreled from the end of the table, snatching their attention.

The green-eyed monster once more took hold while watching Azzan and the woman, each with a child before them, play and laugh. Like a family. He seemed quite happy down there.

"Is that Azzan?" Range asked. "That guy never smiles."

"Well, he's smiling now," someone said, innuendo rich in their words.

Everly swallowed and glanced down at her plate, the sound of that laughter and the playfulness between them haunting. She hadn't realized how much she'd enjoyed his attention until it wasn't there anymore.

"Everly."

She snapped up her head. Managed a weak smile. "Sorry?"

"You confirmed Senator Peterson's coming tomorrow?"

"Yes," she said, scooting up in her chair and slipping back into her campaign manager role. "He'll be here for the concert with Hugh Coton."

"Country," Range groaned. "Never could cure you of that, Stone."

"Nothing to cure, little brother." Stone grinned, rolling his eyes. "So, what now?"

"Dessert in the grand foyer and on the patio by the fire pit. There's a s'mores bar set up for the kids."

"Kids?" Canyon balked. "I want some!"

"Let's raid that thing!" said Canyon's dark-haired friend—Everly couldn't remember his name—as he wrapped an arm around his wife, who was wrangling two bickering boys.

"Move out, ladies!" the largest of the men on Azzan's security team was an African-American man who stood at least six-four, which made his petite white-blond wife seem especially small.

That ache again flared through Everly. They had family, and not just the blood kind. Friends so close they were family. Ever since Grandpa died, her parents had drifted apart.

"They can be a little overwhelming," came the soft voice of Mrs. Metcalfe as she slipped a hand into the crook of Everly's arm.

"Oh, I think it's beautiful." She glided slowly with the older woman behind the rest.

"Me, too," Mrs. Metcalfe breathed. "I want to thank you, again, for all your hard work for Stone. He hasn't had an easy time of it since his father died, but I've never been more proud. If you hadn't approached him, I'm not sure he would have seized this."

"It's my pleasure. I just hope it's enough to get him into office."

"And don't worry about Willow and Azzan."

Everly's gaze flipped to where the two stood by the fire pit, again talking and laughing.

"Those two are more siblings than anything else."

Some siblings. A young girl—maybe ten?—came to Mrs. Metcalfe and clutched her arm, her olive complexion stark against the much fairer older woman. "Ah. Tala, dear." She wrapped the girl close. "Are you ready to make s'mores?"

The girl had Canyon's blue eyes. Pretty. But not as pretty as Azzan's green eyes. The granddaughter and grandmother moved to the fire pit.

To Everly's right stood two groups—Range and Maren, with Ross. Beyond them . . . Azzan and Willow. Harden was there, but he looked like a third wheel. To the far left the wives and children were gathered by a smaller pit, laughing and talking. Their husbands were directly north of them. Standing in a protective perimeter.

And Everly . . .

Alone. As always. She lifted her chin, refusing to feel sorry for herself. She'd done well. The families were happy and the Christmas event was starting off right. Besides, she was used to being an outsider, having been raised in the limelight.

"Excuse me," a little girl said, patting Everly's arm. She held up a wire holder. "Can you help me?"

Saved from pathetic-ness by a tiny beauty with a caramel complexion and brown eyes. "Of course. First, I need to know your name."

The girl swatted away her braided hair with an annoying flick. "Lyric."

"What a pretty name!"

"Thanks. Daddy said Momma was his song, so I'm his lyrics." She skipped alongside Everly to the s'mores bar.

Everly helped her load the marshmallow on it, then lifted a plastic bag of chocolate and graham crackers kits. Her mouth watered, remembering fireside chats with her grandfather. He'd been like a kid with them. A pang hit her. "You know what? I think I want one, too!" She grabbed the supplies for her own and a paper plate.

At the pit, it became obvious this wasn't something new to Lyric, but Everly was glad for the company and distraction. They held the marshmallow over the fire and waited until its edges were almost black. Everly took the wand and knelt.

"Now," she said, pointing to the crackers, "use the crackers and chocolate like a sandwich and clamp them over the mushy marsh—that's it."

Lyric removed hers like a pro. Victory in her eyes, she smiled. Everly did the same, squeezing hers between the graham shell. On a bench, they enjoyed the decadent indulgence, dribbling crumbs and, no doubt, smearing chocolate and marshmallow on their faces. A perfect end to the first half day of the launch. She cleaned the chocolate off Lyric's face, then laughed when the girl smacked her hands as if a job well done, then skipped away.

Everly lifted her gaze, surprised to find Azzan watching.

CHAPTER 6

S HE LOOKED GOOD with chocolate smeared along her cheek. But even better was the laughter she'd shared with Griffin's little girl. It twisted something inside Azzan, seeing her smile like that. It was the closest she'd gotten to carefree abandon, and he had a feeling Everly Sinclair didn't often go there. Reserved. Conservative. If he didn't know better, he'd think her a stiff Brit like a few colleagues. He'd even been accused of that persona by those who didn't know his line of work.

On the second level of the lodge, which was shut down for the night, cloaked in shadows, quiet, and the crackling of the massive fireplace in the middle of the foyer, Azzan glanced down the hall. Doors closed. No obvious conversation or approach. Then checked the foyer, the desk clerk, who stood and moved to the coffee bar to pour himself a drink.

Azzan's gaze hit the exposed crossbeams of the foyer that gave the place a rustic feel . . . and provided a Parkour-loving freak like himself an opportunity.

One not to be refused.

With a skip, he sprinted at the ledge. Toed it. Sailed out over the open foyer and threw himself at the beam. With a slap, he caught it, allowed the momentum to swing him down and under. Then back. He released it, arcing up and catching the slanted, upper beam to stop himself. With an effortless ease, he dropped onto the lower beam. Crouched there.

Something about this, about being high up, drenched him with adrenaline but also balanced him. Brought equilibrium. Forced him to shut out thoughts and . . . focus. Lowering himself onto the ledge, he sat with his legs dangling and faced the wall-to-ceiling windows that looked out and up the hillside. Counted the red glints of his security system. Not visible from the ground. Only those who knew where to look would see evidence of his system. A dozen of them littered around the trees, giving him awareness of his surrounding that went beyond instinct and sending a signal to his watch.

It'd never work with her.

Roughing a hand over his face, Azzan reminded himself Canyon would add a hole to his head if he even tried.

But who was she that she'd even want to be a campaign manager? And the way she held herself, the way she conducted herself—it spoke of more than just a college girl trying to make her way. Tapping his fingers lightly on the rough-hewn beam, he probably should check into her. Run her name. Get her credentials. Don't take it on Stone's word. Or Canyon's. In Azzan's previous line of work, doing that got you killed. So, he needed to check her legend. Interview her friends—casually, of course. Maren seemed like a watchdog. Harden was slimy, trying to steal her glory. Ross, yeah—Azzan didn't like him. He seemed too interested in her, though he played it off.

Tomorrow was registration and cocktails. Perfect time—

Azzan stilled. His gaze struck a dark spot in the trees. Pitch black draped with snow. But black. His gaze skidded around the trees, then flipped back to the spot. Six feet to the right, a red dot winked out.

Someone's out there . . .

Voices came from below.

Azzan hopped to his feet, balancing on the six-inch beam, then lowered himself to a crouch. Fingers on the wood, he monitored two men emerging from a side hall. Kind of late for drinks at nearly two a.m. But some people needed that.

Only these two weren't drunk. And they weren't coming from the direction of the bar. From the side parking lot.

Harden sauntered in, talking low with another man, but with shadows and being above them, he couldn't see the man's face. Turning a circle as they crossed the lobby to the elevator, Azzan noted the man's movement—a bit awkward. Arthritis maybe. Or an old injury. Build—slight belly bulge, rounded shoulders, drooped neck. Definitely older, despite the dark hair. Dye.

As the elevator climbed to the second level, Azzan hurried to the end of the beam, turned his back to the open space and hopped into the air.

He caught the beam and swung to the side. He leaped over to the fireplace and dug his fingers between the stones, a slippery venture that. With a hop to the wall, he lightly toed it and dropped to the floor. Slipping out the door into the frigid weather, he heard the elevator ding. In a light jog, he made his way up to the trees to find out what was happening with the security system.

Snow crunched beneath his feet and he pushed, light and quick, up the hill. He cringed at the noise his weight made and cursed himself for becoming sloppy. Using the limbs for steps, he climbed to the perimeter alarm.

His comms piece buzzed in his ear. He smirked and pressed it. "Go ahead," he subvocalized.

"Motion detected in the trees," Colton said, his voice groggy. "Got an alarm."

"When?"

"Just now."

"Copy," Azzan said. "It's me. Someone killed two sensors." The device was intact. No damage. He slid down the tree and dropped onto the forest litter.

"How'd they do that and not set it off?"

"That's what I'd—"

A black blur came at him.

Azzan ducked. Heard the crack of the tree behind him. Dove into the legs of the man. They went down. An assault of fists on his head and neck forced him to roll away and leap to his feet—even as he turned to face the attacker, a large black boot came at his face. Nailed him.

The hit spun him around, which he used to his advantage. Thrust out his leg and swiped his attacker's. Then flung himself and threw a punch.

Face concealed behind a balaclava, the man ducked but threw an uppercut at Azzan. Pounded his gut. Knocked the air out of him. Another fist came at his face. He caught and twisted it. The man head-butted him.

Stumbling back, Azzan fought the blur in his vision. Felt the stream of warmth along his temple. In the distance, he heard shouts. His name called.

Angry, he roared and lunged forward.

The man swung at him.

Rough, the branch scraped his cheek. Thudded against his head. Hollowed his hearing.

Azzan went to a knee. Blinking. Heard the rapid retreat of the attacker's boots. And the frantic call of his friends. Rage tore through him. He slammed both fists into the ground with a howl. No matter how hard he tried, no matter the good he'd done in the last few years, his past always found him.

BESIDE HER STOOD a mountain of a man named Colton Neeley with some type of binoculars pressed to his face. It was hard not to notice the weapon holstered on his thigh or the raw intensity that seemed to melt the snow beneath his feet.

Everly tugged the wrap tighter around her shoulders, shivering from what she'd seen—Azzan hopping from a beam a dozen feet in the air, then sprinting out into the night. And what she hadn't seen—Azzan returning. She rushed to the doors, worry clutching at her as minutes ticked by. Next thing she knew, the men he'd brought in, Canyon's team, came barreling around the corner from the rooms wing, weapons held low and faces taut with concern.

"Are y'all always . . . *prepared* like that?" she asked.

He didn't move. "Most times."

Wasn't it taking too long?

Everly swallowed and looked up at Colton. She only reached the man's shoulder. *Intimidating* didn't come close. Then again, his intimidation had nothing on what Azzan did to her.

"Here they come," Colton said, his squared shoulders softening—no, releasing tension. This man wasn't soft. "Aladdin's with them. It's good."

"Aladdin?"

Colton lowered the binoculars and smiled. "Nickname goes way back."

Her gaze shifted to where four shapes seeped from the darkness, crossing into the wan light of the lodge. Flurries lazily swirled around Azzan, whose expression was icy and hard. Then his gaze hit hers.

He blinked. His flint facade faltered, then knotted into anger.

Everly stepped back, unsure what that meant.

The manager and assistant manager rushed into the night. "Is everything okay?"

"No," Canyon bit out. "Someone attacked our security chief. We need to talk."

Attacked? Everly eyed Azzan as he strode past her, his gaze skidding in her direction but never quite meeting her.

Colton and Griffin guided Everly inside, and though she felt prodded along, she was too stricken at the thought of Azzan being attacked to argue.

"We need to get your security team up and debrief," Max said, taking charge. "In the campaign conference room." He nodded to the manager, who hurried away to comply.

Hands planted on his belt, Azzan stared at the floor. Scrapes along the planes of his face were red and dribbling blood, which traced his jaw—the muscle flexing tight—and splatted his jacket. A knot at his temple pushed into his brow, thickening it. What she saw in his face, in his expression and eyes, scared her. An anger so fierce, so virulent, she dared not tempt it.

Everly took a step back.

"You okay?" Colton asked, touching her shoulder.

"Sure," Everly said, with a weak smile.

"Why are you out here?" Griffin asked.

"I . . . I saw Azzan sprint outside."

Max edged in. "Did you see anyone else out there besides Lygos?"

Lygos. Aladdin. How many names did he have? "No," Everly said with a slight shake of her head. "I didn't see anything once he went into the trees."

"C'mon,' Max said as he started toward the conference rooms, where their office had been set up. "Let's get some coffee brewing and talk this out."

"You don't have to come," Griffin said to her softly.

"I—" Everly's gaze hit Azzan, only to find him looking away. "I don't think I could sleep. This is my campaign. And if Stone—"

"Stone's asleep," Canyon said. "I told his detail, but I also gave orders he wasn't to be disturbed. At this point, he's not in danger, so we'll figure out what happened, then where to go from here."

Everly took in a slow breath. "So, you don't think this is . . . a threat?"

Something shifted in Azzan's face, his cheek twitching, then he strode toward the office.

"No," Canyon said. "Probably not." He nodded at her. "Go ahead and get some rest. We'll call you if we need you."

That sounded a lot like a dismissal. But she wasn't ready to surrender control. "Thanks, but if you don't object, I'd like to sit in on this. It's my first campaign, and I'd"—she shook her head and shuddered, memories of Grandpa assailing her—"never forgive myself if something happened simply because I chose sleep over the safety of my candidate."

Canyon gave her a nod, glanced to Colton. "Stick close."

"Like glue." Colton smiled down at her, his blue eyes glinting in amusement as they started to the room. "But I have a feeling it's not me she wants close."

PRIDE GOETH BEFORE *a fall.*

Azzan just prayed that Everly didn't see this as a failure on his part. He snorted—she should. He definitely did. They'd spent the better part of an hour going over, in detail, what happened. No, he didn't get a good look. No, he didn't know who attacked him. Could he identify the person if he came upon them again? Maybe. Was he mad—heck yeah.

But the crux was this: whoever was here, whoever had hit in the dead of night was here because of one person: Azzan.

His past. His hand-bloodied past was rearing its ugly head. And putting Ever—everyone at risk.

"Well, you should get that taken care of," Max said, pointing to Azzan's face. "I'll call in some more guys tomorrow to help with security."

"I think we can get some high-tech equipment," Griffin said. "I've got some buddies who owe me favors."

"Everyone owes you," Max groused.

"Including you, Frogman." Rumbling laughter filled the room.

"What about Stone?" Colton asked.

"He's a former sheriff," Max said. "He can handle himself if needed."

The guys nodded.

"I'll get a first aid kit," Everly said, slipping out of the room.

Azzan rushed to the door and closed it behind her. Turned to the guys. "This is about me."

Max frowned. "Say again?"

"Me—this attack." He shook his head. "Gotta be. Why else would someone attack and take down security?"

"Because my brother's running for governor?" Canyon snickered.

With a snort, Azzan asked, "How many politicians have you seen taken out?"

"Not enough," Griffin laughed, then swallowed his smile as he met Canyon's gaze. "No offense."

"Seriously—this is a legit threat. The guy who hit me knew Krav. Knew how to fight. It's me. Someone from my past coming to settle a score." He drew in a long breath, then let it out, sliding his hands over his face and head.

"Okay," Colton said calmly. "Let's roll that die you're holding—who? And why now? There's a whole lot of ammo"—he motioned around the room—"protecting you, protecting this location."

"Valid point, but men like me take that as a challenge. It's not a threat. It's an invitation." He paced, arms folded as he tugged the winter beanie down over his ears. "I don't want anyone getting hurt because of me. If she finds out—"

"Hold up," Max said with a twinge of confusion in his dark brows. "*She?*"

"*Everly,*" Canyon growled. "I told you—"

A knock sounded on the door.

In a visual standoff with Canyon, Azzan waited as the door

opened.

"I found one," Everly said quietly.

Tearing his gaze away, Azzan moved to the table where gift bags were neatly arranged in bins for registration, which would happen tomorrow. He glanced at his watch. In four hours.

He'd put her in danger. Put Stone in danger. All of them. This is why he avoided social things. This is why he limited his time with Piper and the kids. It wasn't because he was anti-social. But it seemed with the prices on his head, he was anti-survival for those he cared about.

"Hey." Her voice was soft, yet shrieking against his condemnation. "They, um, left, but I have this. If you need it."

He glanced at the first-aid kit in her hand. She opened it, then pulled out a sterilized wipe. When she held it out, he could only stare at it, his will violently opposed to the thoughts of her here. The wish that she'd take that cloth—

Cold streaked the side of his face. He stared into her eyes as she swiped it along his face gently. A hint of a smile tweaked her lips, and he warned himself to stay put. If she had any idea who she was tending, she'd drop it and run. Instead, she persisted, applying more pressure. Though it stung along the cuts and scrapes, he didn't wince.

"Does it hurt?"

He wouldn't feel even if she punched him. Her touch was soothing, right. His mind—he was losing his mind!

Azzan took the box, his fingers grazing hers, surprised at how warm they were. And soft. His gaze hit hers.

Eyes wide and pleading, she held his stare. "You scared me," she breathed, eyes melting with tears.

A hand cupped her face. His hand. Heart thundering like an AK-47. "I never want to do that," he whispered, his words cracked and hoarse against the raw emotion tightening his chest. He smoothed back her black hair and something in him roared at her reaction. The intake of breath. The parting of her cranberry lips.

Like a tow line, she drew him in. Felt her nervous breath along his jaw. But a whisper hung between them. Each of her jagged breaths begging him closer. Felt the silkiness of her cheek, stained with a blush that brightened her eyes and face. So beautiful. He aimed for those lips. Ached to taste their sweetness.

Wave off!

He probed her golden eyes. Knew she'd let him. Knew he wanted to.

A fraction closer.

She shuddered the next breath.

You'll get her killed.

Azzan hung his head. Managed a weak and pathetic, "Sorry." And walked out.

CHAPTER 7

"**H**EARD THERE WAS some excitement last night."

Everly flinched as Maren slid up next to her at the registration table. She felt the heat climbing into her face. How had Maren found out about Azzan and her?

"Saw Mr. Security Chief—his face is scratched up. Did you see it?"

Up close and very personal. "Yeah." Along with his warmed breath caressing her cheek when he held her for those agonizing seconds. Those green eyes warned how much he wanted to kiss her.

"Did they catch the guy?" Maren asked, looking sharp and snazzy in a navy business suit.

Everly twitched herself back to reality. Right. "No. They said they searched but there was no sign. They're calling in more security."

"Are you worried someone will try to do something—"

"No!" Everly snapped, straightening her blazer as she smiled at a group coming toward them. "And we aren't going to bring it up again," she hissed, then turned to the newcomers. "Thank you for coming out, Representative Hascomb. Can I get you to sign in here?" She walked through the registration line where he, his wife and three children received goodie bags, a booklet on Stone Metcalfe, as well as a room of swag gear donated by the Marshall Vaughn Foundation. "There are several activities happening before you head home for Christmas—including a cocktail party, a small fair with activities for the children, skiing, and then the big gala."

She repeated the spiel several times, as did Ross, Harden, and Maren. By lunchtime, most guests were checked in and either eating lunch or resting up for the party this evening. Everly tried not to let the weight of a threat press on her mood or ability to pull this off. She would make Grandpa proud. Even if she couldn't convince the most gorgeous guy on the planet to kiss her, she would convince constituents to put Stone in the Governor's mansion.

Down the hall came Canyon's beautiful sister. "How're you doing?"

Everly smiled. "Surviving." She glanced at the registration table, that now had a dozen or more people huddled around it, her team handling the influx well. "I think at least eighty percent are checked in with no hiccups."

"Good," Willow leaned in with a rueful smile. "But I meant after last night's adventure."

"Oh." Everly could not stop the blush if she tried. "A little rattled, but they're handling things, and I trust hi—them, so . . ." She shrugged.

Willow smirked, her pink lips twisting in apparent understanding. "I meant with the security, not with the mysterious Aladdin."

Mouth gaping, Everly drew back.

Willow laughed and pulled her into a hug. "You are so transparent." She released her, then squinted. "Has he kissed you yet?"

Frustration coiled in a knotted, tangled attraction, confusion, and who-knows-what-else, along her heart. "Excuse me. I need to make sure we transition to lunch."

"He never kisses anyone, Everly," Willow called quietly.

The words chased her to the table, and she was grateful for the din of conversation that drowned Willow's words. What did it mean that Willow knew he didn't kiss? Was it true? Why?

And where was he? It was nearly lunch and she hadn't seen him yet. Some security chief.

Not fair. He'd been beaten up last night and probably was out there, searching the trees again. Her gaze drifted to the large, plate-glass windows. Were they in danger?

". . . Harden told us he had that arranged," a woman's voice broke through Everly's thoughts.

She turned to find Delegate Northam with her husband and adult son. "I'm sorry," Everly said. "What did Harden say he'd arranged?"

"Oh," the woman eyed Everly, seemingly unsure whether she should communicate with her.

"Everly Sinclair." She offered her hand in greeting. "I'm Stone Metcalfe's campaign manager."

The woman frowned. Glanced at the men with her. "I thought Harden said he was."

Maren snorted—loudly. "He wishes!"

"Harden works with my team, yes," Everly said. "How can I help you?"

"Oh, it's nothing big. He'd just said we'd have a ski package while we were here."

Apparently, this woman was too busy to read her invitation. "Of course. It's all included in the weekend's activities. Skiing is tomorrow, with a warm meal provided afterward. This evening is a meet and greet."

"Wonderful! It was so nice of you to work with him on that."

Irritation stirred in her stomach as she smiled and promised herself she'd kill Harden later. "Thank you. If you follow Ross, he'll walk you through the registration for your loot bags and gear."

"I am going to strangle that guy," Maren growled in her ears as they watched the family saunter off. "And what is it with that woman that she treated you like a half-naked slave?"

Everly laughed. "Shh."

"Ms. Sinclair?"

Everly turned to a courier, who stood with a next-day envelope. She signed for it, then asked him to wait. From her purse, she grabbed a bill and handed him the tip. "Thank you!"

"Hey," Maren said. "Tonight during the cocktail party, can we dance?"

Tearing open the easy strip of the envelope, Everly shrugged. "Why would I care, as long as we're available to the guests?"

"Just making sure?"

"Aha." Dropping the cardboard strip in the trash, she pulled out a small padded envelope. After discarding the bigger one, she slid her finger under the sealed flap. "So this is about Canyon's brother, huh?"

"Can I help it if he has those gorgeous blue eyes? And he's in the service."

"Coast Guard, right?"

Maren's eyes gleamed.

Laughing, Everly glanced into the envelope.

And dropped it. Stepped back, feeling a horrible surge of dread that smacked her palms and gut at the same time. Nausea swirled. As she stared at the petals dancing on the air and landing in a macabre pattern on the floor.

COCKTAIL PARTIES WERE an opportunity for the weak to get drunk, the chatty to burn off ears, and introverts to die a long, painful death.

And for Azzan to watch Everly Sinclair.

He hadn't been able to forget that near kiss. Nor get out of his head how willing she'd been. How willing he'd been to break every code and vow he'd made about getting close. He'd allowed a relationship with Piper and the kids only because Colton was a sniper and a bear of a guy. And Piper had served her two years in the Israeli Defense Force before coming to America.

But Everly . . .

What was wrong with him?

He'd seen what happened earlier, the shock of that envelope and her lightning-fast recovery when Stone happened upon her. She'd expertly diverted everyone to the lunch buffet to draw attention.

Was it his imagination, or was she clinging to the table a lot tonight as she stood at the back, the guests mingling, laughing, talking? The Big Band she'd hired sent music through the room, drawing men and their trophy wives—for the most part—onto the dance floor.

Max had brought in another dozen men, all in vantage positions, watching the perimeter of the lodge. Stone's security detail requested a half-dozen more suits. All in all, it should feel more secure. But it just felt like a death trap to Azzan.

"Do me a favor?"

Azzan straightened at Stone's voice. "Anything."

"Stay close to her."

Frowning betrayed him. "Her?"

Stone smirked. "Everyone's worried about me, but I'm worried about her."

"Her." Again, Azzan refused to believe who he meant.

"Everly is a strong woman, but . . ." Stone glanced at the drink in his hand. "She's been through a lot with what happened to her grandfather. And honestly?" He slid a gaze in Everly's direction. "I can tell she's rattled. You being attacked really hit her. She's afraid this thing will end with someone hurt or injured, and that would devastate her."

"Might devastate you," Azzan said.

"I have experience and my own skillset protecting me. She has us, and I don't want her hurt."

"Understood."

Stone considered him for several long seconds. "I hope so."

Though Azzan got the warning loud and clear, he kept his expression impassive as the older guy moved off. Fisting his hands, he stood there watching the revelry, hating politics more than ever. This wasn't his scene. His gaze traced the ceiling of the grand room, wishing it had beams like the lobby.

When the music slowed, Willow appeared. "Dance with me, Carpet Boy."

Azzan snorted. "You know I don't."

She took his hand. "Which is why you will." Though she tugged him to follow, he planted his feet. "Oh, come. You're going to draw attention."

"I think you're the one doing that."

"And you're guilty by association, so c'mon." She yanked again.

With a huff, Azzan followed her to the side, where they found room.

She turned and placed a hand on his shoulder and the other in his palm. "Quite the scratches. Feel all manly now?"

"I felt more when I was trying to put the guy's nose through his gray matter."

"Now, there's the Aladdin I know." She smiled and swayed, a comfortable rhythm that did nothing to stir any attraction. It just wasn't like that with them.

But it did make him wish another woman was in his arms.

"Everly's pretty shaken up."

"Uh huh."

Her blue eyes held his. Then she frowned.

"What?"

"You did your research on her, right?"

Azzan scanned the crowd. He should be pacing and assessing, not dancing. Not thinking through the mistake of avoiding digging into Everly's background.

"You didn't," Willow marveled. "Why ever not?"

"I have work to do," he said, releasing her.

But she tightened her grip on his hand. "Why?"

Grinding his jaw, he met her gaze. Glowered. Let his ire rise.

Willow slowly released him and stared up at him, bewildered. "You research *everyone*. You're anal about it."

How was he to explain there were some things he didn't want to learn from a dossier? That he had this inkling Everly Sinclair was so much more than a conglomerate of dates and locations, that she was worth more than invading her past in that way?

"Azzan, research. You need to. On this one, I promise."

Hesitation held him there for a second too long. "Why?"

This time, Willow hesitated. "You honestly don't know?" She breathed through a laugh. "You really like her, don't you?"

His fingers curled into fists. "I'm here for a job."

Slowly, her head began a languorous shake. "No," Willow said, "it's much more than that." She glanced across the room to Everly. "She's more than that to you. I asked her if you'd kissed her and she crazy-blushed."

"I haven't."

"But you wanted to?"

Arms folded over her chest, Everly stayed near the table. In the corner. The table a barrier. Her arms a barrier. What'd happened? What changed her open demeanor? The good guy on her team, Ross, approached her. Insisted she join him for a dance. Everly refused, but Ross proved persuasive. Pulled her onto the floor as the new song began. A green cord of jealousy strapped Azzan's chest like a tourniquet to a bleeding wound.

Willow took his hands again. Moved him around the room.

"You really like her."

He snapped out of it. "What are you doing, Willow?"

"Trying—as I have been for years—to crack the hardest nut on my brother's team."

"It's a waste of time."

A smile slowly curved up the side of her mouth. "Oh, I don't know about that."

They were nearly in the middle, people on all sides. He hated it. The crowds. Couldn't assess. Couldn't—

Willow let go of his hand.

"Willow, a dance?"

"I'd love to Ross," she said, swinging into the other man's arms.

Azzan turned—right to Everly.

Willow nudged him closer. "Change partners!" She whirled away with Ross.

Tentatively, he took Everly's hand, heat coating his shoulders when she stepped into him. He slid a hand around her waist, ignoring—or trying—the sloping of her hip.

"I . . ." Her face went red. "I wouldn't have! He tricked me."

"We were ambushed," he agreed as he pulled her closer, glad—annoyed—when she hooked her hand over his shoulder.

Her fingers lifted from there and traced his cheek. "Scratches don't look as bad today."

Did she have any idea what her touch did to him?

"I've had worse."

Her gaze rose to his brow where he bore a scar. "Apparently. Where did you get it?"

Wrong course of conversation. "Vicious cat."

She smiled. "Never did like them. Give me a Golden Retriever any day."

"Loyal and beautiful." Like her.

"Exactly." Her chin lifted as she laughed.

There was a nice timbre to her laughter. He wanted to see more light dance in her eyes. She deserved it. Somehow, he knew she did—and that he'd never deserve *her*. So beautiful and innocent. Untouched by war or combat. Reality sucked at times like this. Because a woman of her caliber, when she found out who he was, what he'd done . . . she'd do the sensible, sane thing and walk.

The song ended and, as if a foretelling of his words, they drew apart to offer applause.

Clapping, Everly went rigid.

Azzan tensed, followed her gaze to the door where an entourage arrived. In the center, a man with an American flag pin. Around him four armed security. He turned back to her. "What?"

Shadows darkened her eyes. Held her clasped hands before her mouth.

He touched the small of her back. "Everly." Alarm spread through him as he once more considered the newcomers, who were now being welcomed by that punk guy always stealing Everly's glory.

Joy vacated her expression, leaving in its chilled wake, grief. Emptiness. She was going pale as she watched the five cross the room to Stone.

He stepped in front of her, breaking her line of sight. "*Everly.*"

Finally, her gaze shifted. Snapped to his. A breath of a smile that neither creased the edges of her mouth or her eyes appeared, like something translucent, unable to conceal what really lay beneath. "Sorry." The word choked on air. Fell dead between them.

Something primal awoke in him. "What's wrong?" The question startled him because it felt a lot more like *Who do I need to kill?*

CHAPTER 8

DEATH ROSE ON the shadows and trailed a chilling wake as it followed the senator.

Everly shook herself free of the icy hand that traced her spine. Realized the green eyes staring at her were rimmed in alarm and dangerous ferocity.

It startled her. But that look, that protectiveness that seemed inherent in his expression, stirred longing, too.

Give it up. He walked out once already.

She ran a hand along the back of her neck. "It's nobody—I mean, sorry." Of course it was someone! She swallowed her nerves and the lies. Shook her head. "I . . . it's Senator Peterson. Majority leader." She smiled, unable to look in that direction again, afraid it would once more awaken the haunting demons of that wretched night that stole Grandpa away. She wasn't even sure what it was about those men.

Maren flew at her, barreling her back a step. "Sorry. So sorry. It's him! He came! I can't believe you got him to come."

Bowled over by her friend's enthusiasm, Everly let it overtake the conversation. Put distance between herself and Azzan's ferocity. Somehow, she knew he'd figure out what was wrong. And she didn't want that chapter of her life read again. Not with him.

"I worked hard to get him to come, but he said he wasn't sure."

Maren grabbed her hand and pulled her on. "Thank God you said to save that room for him. Come on! Before Harden steals your thunder."

But even as they crossed the room, Everly felt Azzan's presence. He hadn't liked what he saw and her feigned reassurances hadn't worked. Somehow, she was glad. But she shouldn't be. Because he'd dig. Then he'd know. And he'd treat her different.

"Senator Peterson," Stone said, turning to her as they approached. "This is Everly Sinclair, my campaign manager."

"Ah. Good to meet you, young lady." He shouldered past Harden, who was positively steaming over being nudged out of the conversation. "You drove a hard bargain, but like you, I believe in what Stone is selling."

"Thank you so much for coming, Senator. I'm glad you were able to make time in your schedule to enjoy some relaxing days with Mr. Metcalfe," she said. The man next to Peterson seemed to tense, drawing her attention. He stared hard at Azzan, who did likewise. "Have they gotten you checked in okay?"

"Perfectly. My wife is coming down shortly. I wanted to get in here to talk with Stone about some policy," he said with a mischievous grin.

"Well, I won't get in your way," she said. "You have my number in the emails we exchanged, so if you need anything let me know."

"Be glad to, Darlin'."

She tried not to cringe as she moved away, noting—but trying not to—the way the suited guard eyed her and Azzan.

"I sent him emails, too," Harden said.

"You sound like you're in kindergarten," Maren said with a smirk. "Give it up. Admit it—Everly scored the big fish and you're jealous."

"Not even close," Harden sneered, walking away.

The air suddenly felt stiff and . . . weird. She glanced to Azzan, noticing his hard expression. Again. What was that about?

"Why is that guy even on your team?" He hovered, his gaze probing the crowds until it again found Peterson's team.

"Because he's a good strategist."

"Only when it benefits him," Maren countered.

"And his candidate," Ross added. "Harden's not against cutthroat practices as long as it gets his guy to the top, and takes him along for the ride."

Stay busy. Do something. Just turn away.

"Excuse me," Azzan bit out, then stalked into the middle of the crowd.

Everly moved to the small table in the corner, feeling strangely naked without him hovering. Though the night wore on without anymore of her freak-out moments, she couldn't relax. As the crowds dwindled and voices lowered, the guests settling in at tables to talk, Everly grabbed her wrap and allowed herself to slip outside to breathe.

Leaning on the balcony of the deck that overlooked a fresh blanket of snow, she let her mind close. It was going well. "You'd be proud, Grandpa," she whispered to the swirling flakes. "I wish you were here."

An arm stretched around, the hand holding a smart phone with a picture glowing back at her.

"What?" she pushed up, but felt warm pressure at her back. She glanced over her shoulder, stomach tightening as Azzan leaned in.

"The picture."

She glanced down at it. Sucked in a breath as she saw herself. "That's me—in my office."

He swiped and another picture slid into place.

"Starbucks!" She jerked her gaze to his, heat splashing her belly that he was closer. Their faces inches apart. "It *was* you. You've been stalking me."

Pleased with himself, he nearly smiled. Jutted his jaw to the phone, which was still dangling in front of her. Stubble prickled his jaw. His eyes were pools of confidence. That olive complexion so perfect with his dark hair. He was perfect.

"Ev," he said, nodding her back to the phone.

Heart smiling, she turned—and pulled back, thumping against his chest. Her heat hammering.

"That," he breathed against her bare neck, "was the first time I saw you truly scared."

She gulped the shock over that picture. That was when she'd found the envelope on her windshield with the yellow petals.

"Then I saw it tonight, too."

Panic beat an irregular cadence in her breast. She writhed to get free. To be safe.

His left arm came around, cocooning her.

"Azzan," she whispered, scared yet aching to be held. To be told it'd be okay.

"I won't let anything happen to you," he whispered, his stubble tickling her earlobe as he leaned in. "I promise." He pulled back, then angled around her. "But I need to know what happened in there."

She flinched away. Shifted from him. "It's nothing. Just a . . . bad memory."

"You saw four men in suits and it's a bad memory?"

"Look," she broke away from him. Stood a little straighter. Unable to shake the memory of the envelope the same day he'd breathed along her neck. "I'm not sure if I should be creeped out that you were stalking me or flattered, but—"

"I told you I would always be there." Sincerity bled from his expression. "That you might not see me, but I was there. That's my proof."

Was that all it was? She hated herself for wondering. For hoping he wanted to follow her. Which was downright pervy, wasn't it?

"Thank you. I appreciate that you pay attention." She shifted to the side, closer to the door, wondering if he'd try to stop her. Hating that she felt like a kid trying to get away before being caught stealing from the cookie jar. "But I have work to do."

Even as she strode into the mostly empty cocktail party, Everly wanted to leave. She'd been up late last night because of Azzan's little adventure. She needed rest, so she called it a night.

HE'D BEEN STUPID not to research her. That reaction when he exposed her fear told him to grab a shovel and start digging. Things were getting messy, which made his instincts blaze. That visceral response to the security detail bespoke terror. And she wasn't willing to talk about it.

Trigger #1

Then her heaving response to the near-kiss he'd almost place on her neck told him she wanted him, that she liked him. Trigger #2.

So even with his carefully laid-out explanation of his concern, using those pictures had the opposite reaction. Rather than coming clean, she'd closed up shop and run home.

Time to dig. Azzan tugged out his laptop and worked his way through the encryption and entered her first and last names. Everly Sinclair. A pretty name for a pretty thickheaded woman.

Zero results.

He must've mistyped. Azzan entered the name again.

Two results.

His instinct drew out a baseball bat, ready to assault his attraction to her. It was like seeing a brick wall, protecting the truth. The truth that everyone had more results than that. Keep digging. His next search might net hundreds of results. But he had all night. He typed in her first name.

11,300 results.

Including a movie of the same name about a yakuza sex slave.

"Great," he muttered. Stone knew who she was, it seemed. And Willow did, too. Azzan grabbed his phone. Dialed. "Houston, I have a problem."

"I think I'll start shooting the next person who says that."

"Good thing I called now, before you made that decision."

"Good thing. What can I do for you and your magic carpet."

"You know that's prejudiced, right? I'm half Palestinian, half Israeli."

"Talk about a ticking time bomb. So, what can I do you for?"

"I need a name searched."

"Is that all?"

"Everly Sinclair."

"Oh, like that LeMarque's daughter—no, granddaughter. Yeah, that's right." Keys were clacking. "I loved her name. I know it's weird that I'm a guy and I loved her name, but it just had a ring to it, ya know? And since I deal with letters and numbers—"

"Houston." Frustration made him toss the phone on the desk and hit speaker. He stared down at it. "What're you talking about?"

"Oh, dude, sucks not to be American, huh?" Houston chuckled. "Yeah, so President LeMarque was one of the best presidents in American history. Two terms. One side hated him just because he was so great they knew they wouldn't win the next election, which they didn't. The other side loved their golden boy. But neither could argue how much he helped our country. Dude survived two attacks in office, then when his term ends, almost two years later, he's killed in bed in his own home. Anyway. Secret service agents—dead, his granddaughter died, too. Fell over the staircase balcony in the home." He grunted. "They never caught the assassin."

Pressed lower with each word Houston spoke, Azzan sat on the bed. Shoved his hands over his face, his head, and then his face again. It made sense. Too much sense.

"The LeMarques are like American royalty. When Everly died, the nation mourned. Country's been divided ever since."

"Houston, the results. Send them to me."

"All four of them?"

Azzan deflated. "Yeah."

"Coming your way, A-man. If you need anything else . . ."

"Yeah, thanks. Houston." He reached to press the End button. "Oh. Hey, I'm going to send you a picture. See if you can find something on this guy."

"It'll cost you."

"What about your patriotism you were talking about just now?"

"That doesn't pay the bills, unfortunately. Send it my way. I'll work it over."

"Thanks." He ended the call, sent the photo, then dropped back against the bed. Stared at the ceiling. Held his hand over his eyes, squeezing his temples.

Too much sense.

Abandon the notable name. Use a more generic name. Enter politics.

He snorted. Of course she'd enter politics.

And this quagmire felt like someone set it on fire. Maybe he should hop that magic carpet everyone assumed he had and get out of Dodge. But he laid there, mind swimming in a sea of possibilities. About her. About Peterson. About the man with him. One who resonated with familiarity. The guy was trouble. Azzan knew trouble because *he* was trouble himself. In a crowd, assassins and spies could sniff each other out. Most people had a way about them that fit profiles. Fit personality types. Habits. Hiccups. People like Azzan had the smell of a blank slate slathered with lies.

His phone pinged. Azzan propped on his side, reaching for his phone. The text read:

Initial scan on photo = nothing. I'll keep digging but looks like some serious trouble.

Houston had it right. Because if that man didn't register on facial-recognition databases that his friend could hack from the CIA, NSA, DOD, and NGA, it meant the guy didn't exist. That meant special operators, spies or assassins.

CHAPTER 9

AFTER CHECKING ON the "child center," where more than two dozen kids ranging from infants to pre-teens were engrossed in activities under the instruction of qualified childcare professionals, Everly headed out the side of the lodge where the lift had started running about twenty minutes ago. She glanced at the dark sky and willed it to hold back its bounty. She'd watched the news. There shouldn't be any foul weather until they left in two days.

Two days. Were they seriously halfway through this endeavor?

Laughter barreled out from a group of guys huddled around a line of snowmobiles. They high-fived and clapped each other on the back.

"What's going on?" Everly asked. "Where did those come from?"

"Harden," Maren huffed. "I'm about to freak out—those aren't covered on the insurance plan!"

Irritation squirmed through Everly. "Why can't he stop trying to one-up me and just help make this a success?"

"Hello?" Maren glowered. "Because he's trying to steal this from you."

"I know what he's trying to do, but . . ." Why explain her thoughts? She was a peacemaker with a thick competitive streak.

Her friend considered her. "You look rough."

Everly laughed. "Thanks."

"No, I mean you look like you didn't sleep. Again."

"I got enough," she lied, eyeing the twenty or so men clustered around.

"Dude," Max said, "these are Deep Snow Crossovers with IGX rear suspension."

Which, she guessed, was a good thing. Clearly, the snowmobiles had been a smart move. She'd shared all her ideas with Harden, but he'd kept his to himself. He didn't play fair.

"And Range is taking a machine. I have no idea how to drive those things."

"I don't think the guys would give up one for you anyway," Everly sighed, going to the ski prep area and clamping her boots onto a pair of skis. She waved her friend over. "Maybe he'll let you ride with him."

Mischief sparked in her brown eyes. "You think?"

"Go on. I'll head up the slope and stay with the skiers."

"You sure?"

"Go," Everly teasingly growled, then smiled as her friend scampered over to the others.

When she grabbed some poles and turned, Everly spotted Azzan stalking out of the lodge. She diverted her attention to lining up with a lift basket. Felt it catch the back of her legs and rode up the hillside. At the top, she shimmied into position for the main slope, watching with a smile as Lyric's mom slipped the girl's goggles on and spoke to her. The woman was small, compared to her husband, and her white-blond hair nearly blended with the snow.

"Ms. Sinclair."

To her left, she spied Barton Delaware, an oil magnate from Texas who had long been friends with her family. She felt her stomach squirm, knowing this was one of the few people at the lodge who knew her true identity. "Mr. Delaware, I'm surprised to see you up here on the slopes."

He grunted. "Wanted to ride one of those snowmobiles, but Caprice wanted to ski." He squinted over the pristine setting. "This is a fine thing you're doing. Your grandfather would be proud."

Everly nearly choked on his praise, a lump rising in her throat.

"Tell you the truth," the man said, a strong wind picking up his salt-and-pepper hair and tussling it, "if you say Metcalfe's worth his mettle and my money—"

"He is."

He grinned, dimples poking into his pocked face. "That's all I need to hear."

"I wish others were as easy to convince," she said, eyeing

Representative Hascomb.

"If they were, then you wouldn't have a job." He winked at her again. "I see a lot of Ed in you. More than I ever saw in John."

Edward LeMarque, her grandfather. John LeMarque, her father.

"But you have a whole lot of Melissa, too."

Everly wrinkled her nose. "Hopefully more of Ed."

He barked a laugh. "Could you turn those wiles on Cappy so I can ride one of those machines down there?"

Caprice, his second wife, was the world to him. They had three small children down in the center, and Barton would do anything for that woman. Which was why Everly petitioned his younger wife to bring him.

"You're a good man, to indulge her by skiing. Maybe she'll ride later—"

"I thought you were only twisting arms about your candidate, Everly," Caprice said with a laugh, then kissed her husband.

"I think she's on to something, Cappy," Barton said with a wink as they shuffled to the start line.

"If you win this run, we'll ride." She shoved herself forward, down the slopes.

"Cheater!" Barton's guffaw was swallowed by wind and speed as he pursued his wife.

Not for the first time, Everly was glad she'd hired extras to oversee the desk so she could be out among the guests.

Everly moved into position, aligning her skis. As she stuffed her poles in the snow and lowered her mask, she sensed a presence beside her. She glanced to the man on her right, who had just drawn down the mask over his eyes. He peered at her.

Her heart jolted.

Azzan.

He had challenge set in his eyes. "Race" in his posture.

And she had a whole lot of Ed LeMarque in her veins. She grabbed her poles and stabbed them into the snow, hauling herself over the ledge.

Launching into the crisp air, Everly savored the thrill. The terror of being suspended over a mountain with nothing but oxygen and snow between her and death. She leaned into the free-fall, then landed with a thump against the packed snow. Wind tore at her as she slalomed down the mountain.

She didn't dare turn away from the deadly obstacle course in front of her, but Everly saw the blur of black racing her down the mountain. She stabbed the earth and pulled to pick up momentum. Angled around a curve. Avoided a copse of pine trees.

He was edging ahead, but she sighted a spot where—she banked hard right. Cut across his path. He swung to avoid. She corrected her course and sailed toward the end. At the bottom, she spun around just in time to see Azzan whip up alongside her.

She laughed, tugging up her mask.

"So glad you're not competitive," he said.

Laughing more, she resisted the urge to tell him he had no idea.

"Guess it runs in the family."

She snapped a look at him, heart skipping a beat. Then two. Did he know? How had he found out?

"You do the black diamond?"

Stunned at the challenge he laid before her, Everly thought to warn him she'd been raised on the slopes. Every family vacation. Every time her father had to get away, which was often. "I can," she said, deliberately unenthused.

"Scared?"

Only if he found out she was duping him into running it with her. But so few people would. "A little." Because he'd be ticked when she creamed him.

SHE'D BOUGHT THE BAIT. He didn't care about the slope or winning. He just wanted her away from Peterson's group.

They rode the lift up past the blue and on up to the black diamond. She sat there, confident as ever. In fact, he wasn't sure, but she seemed to enjoy this.

"Not afraid of heights?"

She swallowed. "Not most heights."

Okay, what was that? He thought about what he'd read last night—er, early this morning. Everly, the then-fourteen-year-old granddaughter of Ed LeMarque had fallen from the top of a grand staircase, broken her back, and died.

But she was mighty alive for a dead grandchild.

Azzan let his gaze trace the spine of the mountain. This is what he loved. Openness. Breathing space. Being on top of the world, looking down. But the skies. . . "That doesn't look good."

"Weatherman said the storm would come Christmas Eve. We'll be home by then."

"How many weathermen have you known to be accurate all the time?"

"I saw, you know." She waited as the lift leveled off, then hopped from the seat, shuffling aside in case someone was behind them. Which there wasn't.

Caught off guard by her comment, he did the same. "Saw what?"

"You." She peered out over the mountain. "The night you were attacked—before you went out. I saw you on the beams."

Azzan dropped his gaze for some reason. He wasn't sure why, but it made him feel weird that she'd seen that.

"You're graceful." She sighed. "I couldn't do that, sit on the beams, then hop off."

They plodded to the start point. "Most people can't. I train long and hard to do what I do."

She peered down the steep descent. "You sure you want to do this?"

"Chickening out?" he asked with a grin as he lowered his mask.

"You said that to the wrong girl." Everly gripped her poles.

"Keep it fair. On three—"

"Where's the fun in that?" Everly launched herself forward.

Throwing himself into the air, Azzan was determined not to let her win. He wasn't one of those guys who let the girl win so she'd feel better. That served nobody any good, and he was pretty sure it'd tick Everly off.

The freefall on the lower slope didn't come close to this one. Azzan kept his eye on her as she sailed through the air. For a second, he took in the serenity of the mountain, the gray clouds. That was going to be a problem. He could feel it.

Wind tore at his jacket, threatening to pitch him into the earth for defying gravity. But he controlled his descent. Let his skis kiss the snow. Then leaned farther forward to force momentum to carry him faster.

Like lightning, Azzan bolted past her.

But as they'd neared a rocky spot, he'd seen something. Too tricky to navigate with distraction. Azzan returned his attention to the dangerous ledge that whipped them to the left, then the right around a copse. Rocks dared them to make a mistake.

Black movement to his right. Azzan glanced there. What . . .?

Everly blurred past him, taking a sharp curve in a full squat. She came up out of it and worked her skis and poles to gain speed.

For the next curve, she . . . wasn't she going too fast?

His heart thudded. He sped up, watching as she went into that curve.

Too much, too much!

In a squat, she tilted to the side and skidded, gouging a crevasse through the snow. Azzan aimed for her, slowing as hard as he could. "Everly!"

She rolled onto her back and laughed, shaking her head.

"I guess you're not hurt."

She removed her mask and shook it out with a huff. "Just my pride." She sat up and moved to the rocky outcropping that wasn't part of the course, to be safe in case other skiers were coming down. "I've done that course a hundred times and never miscalculated that one."

He nodded. "Wait." He frowned at her. "A hundred times?"

Everly laughed again, dangling her arms over her legs as she traced their surroundings. "My . . . grandfather loved Bexar-Wolfe Lodge. We used to come here all the time . . ."

"Until he died." Though he gave away nothing in his expression, he saw the question rise and fall in hers.

"A lot of things, favorites, died with him." She set her mask on her head, but didn't cover her eyes. She seemed content to sit here.

They sat in the quiet of the mountain, nothing between them but the cold and thin oxygen. And he liked it. A lot. He shouldn't. He had a job and his very existence meant trouble. Especially that guard. He wasn't sure who he was, but there was something very familiar about him.

"All my life... my entire life was absorbed in secrecy, in privilege that kept me locked away from people and normalcy," Everly said. "That changed when he died."

Changed. That was interesting.

She huffed. Looked at him. "Do you know, Azzan?"

This wasn't how it worked. It wasn't how it should work. On a job, he didn't reveal what he knew. He kept it close. Worked his angles. He just prayed she wasn't asking what he thought she was asking.

"Do you know who I am, really?" Gold eyes sparked at him. The heavy sky and its light seemed to trace the flecks that dotted her nose and rosy cheeks.

Somehow, telling her felt like it'd be the same kind of death she had with her grandfather. That it'd change him. Change them.

"I want you to know," she whispered. Then started, surprised at her own words. She looked away, down. Shook out her goggles and started to stand. "Never—"

He caught her. Drew her back down. Stared into those eyes again. "I know."

Desperation wormed through her face. "What . . . what do you know?"

He hated this. Hated that he might have the wrong answer. That the wrong answer could turn her away and inflict more hurt.

Who was he kidding? Any answer he gave would hurt her. Because he understood her. Understood what that question meant to her.

Eagerness replaced desperation that glowed against her freckles. "Say it," Everly said. "Say my name."

"Promise me one thing first."

Hesitation guarded her. "Okay."

"Tell me what was in the envelope."

She gulped. Stared at the snow. Grief and agony wrestled through her pretty features, snow-dampened hair hanging in stringy vines around her face. So pretty. So alluring.

She wouldn't tell him. Whatever that envelope held was too painful. Too much "her" to hand to a near-stranger.

"Petals," she mumbled. Everly closed her eyes. Shook her head.

As in flower petals? "Why would they upset you?"

Watery eyes came to his and resistance played through her features, wrestling for control. "Say it." Pleading and need drew him nearer. Lips parted, she waited.

"Everly Sinclair . . ." Name this name and he changed everything. It could get her killed. Or him. But holding it back any longer might kill him anyway because he saw the eagerness, the desperation to be named, to be known.

Why? Was he so willing to break his rules for her? Why did he want to go to the ends of the earth for this beguiling woman? What was it about her? He didn't understand. Didn't know how she'd forced her way past his armor and dug into his heart.

The eagerness fading, she began to shrink away.

And it hurt him because it hurt her. "LeMarque."

She drew up with a sharp intake. A breath shuddered its warm relief. "You know."

"Is that a good thing?"

"Yeah," she said with an airy laugh, then frowned. "Usually it's not, but yeah . . . I wanted you to know."

"And the petals?"

She blinked and started to look away, but he lifted her chin to him.

"I'm here. There's nothing to fear." He wanted to kiss her. Needed to.

A weak smile. "It's just . . . a painful reminder. Maybe a threat."

Azzan tensed. "A threat?"

She stayed close, as if drawing comfort from his presence, and that was a change. For anyone to seek that from him. To find it. "I had gone down to the kitchen for water. I used to have bad dreams a lot," she said shaking her head. "When I came back upstairs, there was this round table with a gorgeous bouquet of flowers that sat between my bedroom and Grandpa's. I'd just rounded the corner when I saw a dark shape rush from Grandpa's room"—she swallowed hard—"he plowed right into me, somehow shoving me over the rail. Maybe he pushed me, I don't know. I can't remember. What I do recall is lying on the floor in the foyer, staring up as petals rained down. That table above—the flowers were knocked over. Petals rained down. That is the last thing I saw before waking in the hospital."

"With a broken back."

She nodded, then looked down toward the lodge. "Three surgeries and a year of physical therapy got me back up walking. Only in the last couple of years have I tackled sports."

"And you just did the Black with me."

She laughed. "I failed, if you'll recall."

"You read the situation and prevented a tragedy."

"You're sweet."

Now, he laughed. "You have no idea how wrong you are." He roughed a hand over his head.

She squinted up at him. "I can't figure you out, Azzan Yasir. When you first arrived, I was sure you were a jerk."

"I am."

"But then you diverted Harden that first meeting."

"He's a jerk, too."

"But you're not a coward," she said. "Like that assassin who killed Grandpa."

Azzan recoiled internally.

"We were very close, my grandfather and I." Grief darkened her features. "He taught me so much. Said I'd be the next president. I never wanted that—the limelight we had while he was in office was suffocating enough, but I loved the thrill of the run for office. He was training me. I was closer to him than I am my own father."

Dying with each word, realizing he would never be to this woman what he had begun to entertain, Azzan knew he must extricate himself from her life. Before it was too late.

"He didn't even face my grandfather," she said softly. "Just shot him in his sleep. What kind of man does that, murders for a living?"

CHAPTER 10

THOUGH EVERLY RETURNED to the lodge with Azzan, by the time they passed through the heavy insulated glass doors, he wasn't the same man who'd been on the slopes with her. Something happened out there. Something that put distance between them—and a brutal, icy chill.

"Oh thank goodness!" Maren trotted up, hugging a binder, her face twisted in distress.

Everly glanced at Azzan, who strode away without a word. *What did I do?*

"Hey." Maren caught her arm and her attention. "You're not going to believe this."

Everly focused on her friend. On the fact that she had a job to do. A candidate to get launched. "What?" But her gaze stole away to catch Azzan's shadow sliding out of view. Frustration moved her to the office, where she could decompress and realign her priorities.

"I can't believe it," Maren was saying, "I knew he was underhanded, but I never imagined how low he'd stoop." She tossed down the papers on the table. "This time—he went so low, he knocked on the devil's door!"

Surprised at her friend's words, Everly slipped around her to close the door, giving them some privacy. "Calm down and tell me."

With a huff and stuffing her hands on her hips, Maren glowered. "All those phone calls we did from your office? All those letters we mailed?"

Everly drew in a ragged breath, knowing where this was going.

"All those—"

"He took credit."

Maren surged forward, caught her by the shoulders. "Everly.

He's stealing clients! I just overheard Hascomb tell Harden that he'd done such an impressive job on Stone's campaign that he wanted to talk to him."

Frustration clawed at Everly, chasing her into a chair. Elbows on the table, she rubbed her temples.

"What're you going to do?" Maren slumped down on a leather seat beside her. "He can't do this! Not right here under your nose."

"No, he's doing it because he thinks I won't do anything." And he was probably right. It was one thing Grandpa had taught her. Not to defend herself to her critics. To let her reputation and the truth bear itself out.

Maren laughed. "He has another thing coming then." She lifted her eyebrows at Everly. "Right?"

"You know, even the Bible says God is our defender."

"But you're not—" She sucked in a breath. Leaned closer and clutched her arm. "Ev, you can't let this go unanswered.

"I have a campaign to manage, Maren." She stood. "That will speak for itself. And if God wants to straighten out Harden, then He has my full approval, but I can't be distracted with that."

Shaking her head, Maren wore disbelief on her lips like black lipstick. "That's a mistake. If you don't head this off, he'll steal the entire thing from you."

"He won't," Everly said. At least, she hoped not. Stone wasn't a man to be easily duped. He hadn't gotten to where he was, and she hadn't chosen him because he was spineless or witless. "Now, we need to make sure things are set for the dinner buffet when they return from their wintry adventures."

The door opened and Ross ambled in, then hesitated, frowning at Maren. "What's wrong?"

"Please tell her she needs to confront Harden."

Wary eyes slid to Everly, then back to Maren. "You're telling me I should order around our only source of income?"

"I'm telling you that we won't have an income if she doesn't do something about him!"

Everly sighed and shook her head as she slipped out of the office. "Oh, did you need something, Ross?"

"Yeah," he said turning to her. "Mr. Daily wanted to talk to you about the smoking room."

Stopped in the hall, she drew back in confusion. "Smoking room?"

He hesitated. Dodged a look at Maren, then screwed up his face. "Harden apparently told the men ballroom B was a smoking room."

Heat blasted her spine and neck. The lodge manager would have her head. "Harden knows this is a non-smoking hotel. There are laws. Rules." She shoved her hair from her face. "That can't happen." She swallowed. "Okay." She had no choice. Fine. She'd confront him. *God, please go before me and prepare the way . . .*

She fisted her hands, tugging at her long sleeves. "Okay."

"Want us to come with you?" Maren asked—pleaded. No doubt she wanted to see the guy get his comeuppance.

"No. Thank you." Somehow, she did this sort of thing better on her own. Without pressure to perform or satisfy anyone's ego. "In an hour, you can probably find me in the kitchen. With a gallon of rocky road ice cream." She nodded. "Rescue me then."

"I'll join you," Maren said.

With a smile for courage, Everly headed down the hall with low-slung ceilings and just wide enough for a couple of people to pass without colliding. She'd gone for rustic, for notoriety of location, not necessarily for the extravagance, though the Bexar-Wolfe had splashes of that, too.

She turned the corner and felt like she'd slammed into an invisible wall. Coming toward her were Congressman Peterson and his four guards. The one that unseated her courage strode directly in her path and those dead eyes of his warned he would not give her berth.

But neither would she show herself weak or intimidated. No matter how much she really was. Everly smiled at the senator. "Having a good time?"

"Quite," Peterson said. "Heading out now to try the slopes before it gets dark."

"Enjoy yourself," Everly said. "There will be a buffet dinner in the dining hall when you're done."

She pushed herself past the entourage, ignoring the swirling dread that rushed around her as Dead Eyes moved around her. Heart struggling to find a regular rhythm, Everly felt the hall tilt.

The air thin even though she stepped into a wide space. Her ears hollowed. And . . .

Rose petals. Falling rose petals.

Stumbling, she dropped against the wall. Held the chair rail and turned her shoulder into the plaster. Her back to the most likely path of traffic. Closed her eyes, trying to force the image of those pale pink petals floating down on top her.

"You okay?"

With a jerk, she came up straight. Stared right into Azzan's green eyes. "Yes." She glanced over her shoulder. They were gone. Good. "I . . . just stumbled. Tweaked my ankle." A bald-faced lie. "But I'm fine now."

Suspicion crept along the hard planes of his face. His gaze slid down the hall and hung there for several long seconds. And the ferocity, as if a caged panther paced behind those green irises, leapt back to her.

Everly drew herself straight. "Did I upset you?"

"It takes a lot to upset me," he said curtly. "If you'll excuse me."

Wait. What? Everly leaned against the wall, again, this time in defeat. She held up her palms in question. What was that about? What did she do wrong?

Raised voices from the end of the corridor, where she'd been headed, reached her. Harden. What was he doing now?

She stomped on, shutting out the twinge of pain in her ankle and pushed toward the ballroom. There, she found Harden talking animatedly with Mr. Dailey.

"Lord, give me patience . . . or a solid right hook," she muttered as she approached. "Gentlemen," she said, but neither heard her. "*Gentlemen*"—loud this time, capturing their attention, and notably that of a few other men coming their way—"so glad to find you both here. I would have a word."

She motioned them into the room, grateful to find it empty, but also completely arranged in cozy seating groups. Where had Harden gotten all this . . .

No. No no no. He'd removed them from grand foyer, where there was supposed to be a fireside chat tonight with Stone and the representatives. Fuming, she drew the doors shut.

"Is this the smoking room?" one of the men asked.

"Smoking room?" Everly said, tightening her face. "I think there's a mistake. Bexar-Wolfe is a non-smoking facility. I'm sure if you ask the front desk, they can guide you to permissible exterior locations." With that, she closed the door. Turned.

Blazed fire through her glower at Harden.

"Thank you, Miss Sinclair," Mr. Dailey said. "I was very distressed! We have not had smoking inside the lodge in nearly twenty years. Our rating would suffer—"

"Please do not alarm yourself, Mr. Dailey. It was merely a misunderstanding." Everly waited for him to acknowledge the obvious stretch of truth, and with a nod he did so, then left the room.

"You can't lock up over a hundred people in this lodge and expect them not to—"

"They are not locked up in here!" Easy, easy. Calm. Calm. *Don't let him get the best of you, Evvy,* she heard her grandpa's words. "I thought you were struggling for money, Harden."

This new course of conversation made his confrontation-fueled brain stall out. "What?"

"Well," she said, folding her arms. "Had you allowed anyone in here to smoke, the cost of sanitizing the room, possibly replacing the carpets and all furniture pieces would have come out of your pocket." She nodded to where the far wall was missing the upper two feet of wall, allowing for an open concept. "And probably the carpet down the hall as well."

He gaped. "You have to meet their needs—"

"And they have to understand there are limits." She gave a firm nod. "If you'll excuse me, I have to check in on dinner details." Though she started for the door, Everly knew one more thing needed to be said. Maybe two. Over her shoulder, she met Harden's furious gaze. "Put the furniture back, or I'll charge you the labor for that. I gave you an opportunity to partner with me, help Stone. Not try to steal this entire thing out from under me. I've let a lot of your digressions of honor pass, but if you try to go around me again, I'll cancel our contract immediately."

"You can't—"

"You know I can. And I will."

He shoved past her, bumping her shoulder. "You're too quiet

and meek to do that." He snorted and yanked open the door. "You'll never get anywhere in this man's world, Everly. Stop now before you get hurt."

Annoyed, furious, she stared after him, wanting to strangle him. Throw something . . . a chair . . . an entire sofa!—at him. But again her Grandpa's voice sailed from the past, quoting one of his favorite lines from Shakespeare, *"Though she be little, she is fierce."*

CHAPTER 11

C HATTER ROSE AND FELL in regular patterns in the great room. While there were a number of seating groups on the exterior of the area, four sofas hugging the massive fire pit offered a place for Stone Metcalfe to hold court with the politicians. Sitting on the edge of their seats, they were engaged in stiff, earnest conversations.

To his left, a round table for four had been crowded with seven chairs with older children playing board and card games. Younger children were already in their suites, hopefully asleep. At least, that's what Piper had whispered of the twins as she sagged in an arm chair near Sydney Jacobs.

Though Azzan sat with Max, Griffin, Canyon and Colton, his thoughts were elsewhere. Mostly on the face of the guard with Peterson.

I know him. I know those eyes.

But where? The face wasn't recognizable, and with those features, Azzan should be able to recall the man. Having watched from the beams earlier, he'd seen the way the guy had pressed his presence on Everly.

He'd rattled her. So much, she stumbled. Which pulled Azzan from the perch.

He cursed himself. Cursed his inability to stay away from her.

What kind of man does that kind of thing?

For the last twelve years, he had. He was the coward she spoke of. Not in that he killed anyone she knew. But . . . he was an assassin. Had been. Not anymore. He'd traded that job—gladly— when Nightshade offered him a way out. There hadn't been one before them.

Screams assailed the night. That dog barking down the alley. The slap of curtains and fabric doorways beneath the storm's rage. The report of a gun. The thump of a body.

His mom. They'd killed his mom. His late father's Palestinian family blamed her family, Israelis. Israelis blamed his father's family. Azzan decided to find out for himself. Became a Palestinian spy. Got turned by the Israelis when they showed him definitive proof his father's family hired an assassin. One Azzan had hunted right up until he encountered Nightshade in Israel nearly seven years ago.

And this is where he found himself. On the brink of thirty, one answer, many more questions, and loneliness. Bent forward, he rubbed a hand over his knuckles.

"Aladdin."

Though he twitched internally, he mastered his body. Slid his gaze to Max.

"You're uptight tonight. You okay?"

He gave a small nod, gritting his teeth. Because he wouldn't be okay till he figured out that guard. Something wasn't right.

A light flicked off, collapsing the corner of the lodge in darkness. Three shapes merged from the office. Hair rolled at her nape, Everly, still composed and neat in her business attire, headed toward the hub with Ross and Maren.

When he glanced at Stone's powwow, he tensed—Peterson's guard was MIA.

Azzan stood and moved around the fire pit, twitching to make his way to the beams to gain vantage. But that'd be obvious. And distracting. Then Piper would chew him out because McKenna or Ben would want to try to follow him.

As he came around, he spied Peterson and the guard talking about a table of refreshments and drinks. Adjusting his navy knit beanie down over his ears and forehead, he walked to the opposite end of the table. Trolled the treats and finger foods, all of which he'd toss in the bin. Or on the table with the kids. Annoy Piper for giving the kids more sugar. But even as he lifted a small powdered cookie onto the napkin, he noted Canyon cross the room to speak with Everly. What was that about?

Everly seemed to take a large wave head on, almost knocking her back.

Licking the powder from his thumb, Azzan abandoned the

treats in the bin. Passing the senator and guard, he started over to Canyon to find out what was going on. Instead, he clipped this conversation.

"... sure?"

"Positive."

"Is it going to be a problem?"

"Not if I take care of it."

Heat rose through him, as he carried those ominous words with him across the space. What did that mean?

But . . . a wave of realization struck him, slowing him. Making it near impossible to move. The way that guy pressed into Everly. His voice—the slight accent.

Heart racing, thoughts thundering, he lifted his gaze to the person who stepped into his path. Concern bled from gold eyes.

That guard.

No.

"Azzan?"

What were the chances . . .? Couldn't be.

Better not be.

"Aladdin. You with us?"

He met eyes—Max. Concern there too.

"Azzan?"

Blinking, he shook his head. Glanced at the two who'd radiated their concern for him. "Sorry. Something wrong?"

Max smirked. "That's what we both just asked you."

No way he could say anything about the guard. Not yet. Not till he verified. And notified his former handler. "Saw you two talking." He could do this—multitask. "Something wrong?"

"Storm," Max said quietly. "It's building fast. And bad."

"I think we'll be gone before it hits."

"Not sure about that," Max said. "We need to keep an eye on it."

And I need to keep an eye and a weapon on Peterson's guard. Because if it was him . . . *He's here to finish what he started.*

"Azzan." Max waited till their gazes met. "Tell me."

Telegraphing his concern for Everly, he looked at her, then to Max. "We should prep. You know—*in all things prepared.*"

Max lifted his chin a fraction, understanding hitting his granite-like face at the Nightshade motto. "I'll get the guys."

Turning to Everly, he avoided her eyes. Glanced at the schmoozing politicians. "Give us a second." Then he strode to the corner, feeling the wake of rejection he left draw the team. He headed back to his room and accessed it, leaving it open a crack. The team filed in quietly. Azzan scanned the bed, dresser, lamp, windows, looking for anything out of place. He faced the guys, scratching his jaw. Man, he hated this. Didn't want it to be right.

"Go ahead," Max said.

Azzan planted his hands on his belt. "That guard—"

"Peterson's," Griffin rumbled. "He smells like trouble."

"He is," Azzan said. "At least for me. His name is Melker Åkesson."

"An assassin?" Canyon asked, hesitation in his voice and posture.

Another nod. "One of the most notorious of my kind out there. I faced him. Once. Hoped to never do it again."

"Son of a biscuit," Canyon punched to his feet. "I warned you about messing up my brother's launch!"

"This has nothing to do with her," Azzan growled. "And how was I supposed to know an assassin would show up here? It's not like I tagged my location on social media, unlike some people."

"Wait," Max asked, glancing between the two of them. "*Her?*"

Canyon smirked. "He has a thing for the campaign manager, Everly. Told him to beg off until this is over. Not to screw it up."

"I don't have . . . a thing." Their near kiss whacked that lie off his tongue.

"Besides that being one of your worst lies ever," Colton said, scowling, "can we get back to the assassin? Is he that bad?"

Azzan traced the scar that bisected his eyebrow. "This is his mark."

"You sure?" Max asked, his expression severe.

"The eyes are unmistakable. The way he moves. The way he—"

"Recognized you," Canyon said as he sat on the bed and stretched out his legs, crossing them at the ankles. "Knew I'd seen that."

Arms folded, Max stepped forward. "Why is he here?"

"I . . ." Azzan shrugged. "To finish what he started?"

"See, what I'm not understanding is how this guy knew you'd be here."

"I . . . don't know."

"Are we sure he's here for you?" Canyon asked.

"Why else would he be here?" Azzan countered. "That doesn't make sense. And it'd make my knowing him a crater-sized coincidence."

"Yeah. Agreed," Max said, pacing. "But Canyon's got a point—we don't know why he's here, so we need to keep thinking."

It's what they did. Worked out a scenario. Plotted. Planned.

"Let's get DOD in on this. Make some calls. Run his name." Max looked at Canyon. "Think you can get a picture of him to send in?"

"Absolutely."

He focused on Azzan. "Think you need to stay out of sight?"

"Dude's always doing that anyway," Canyon said. "Might have taken him out of assassinating, but can't get the assassin out of him."

"That didn't even make sense," Azzan growled.

"Neither does this guy showing up," Canyon noted as he came off the bed. "And I'm not liking being away from my wife and kids knowing there's an assassin here." He eyed Azzan. "Well, one we don't know."

"Do some of those acrobatic things," Griffin suggested.

"Parkour."

Griffin grinned. "That."

"He's right," Max said. "Stay high. Don't let him get the drop on you—or anyone else."

"Tomorrow's the gala, the big event." Canyon hesitated at the door. "That's a mighty big target. Really, the first time everyone's in the same room at the same time."

A piece of Azzan broke off, the same way it had the night Raiyah died. The night his mother died. He couldn't take losing another . . . "Big target."

CHAPTER 12

THE RAPPING OF a woodpecker drilled Everly awake. She groaned and turned over, stuffing her head under the pillow to drown the noise.

"Everly! Evvy, c'mon." *Rap-rap-rap-rap-rap!* "*Everly!*"

She threw back the pillow and covers, squinting to her alarm clock. It wasn't even six, yet. Growling like the hibernating bear she wanted to be, Everly climbed out of the bed and stuffed her feet in her slipper boots. In her plaid flannel pajamas, she stumped over to the door. Slammed back the locks, then the door. "What?" she hissed—but Maren plowed in. "Have you seen?"

Squinting, annoyed at being awakened before six, she closed the door and stared at her friend. "What? I can barely see you right now."

With a rip of the blinds cord, Maren snapped up the blinds until they vanished below a small fabric valance. She stabbed both hands like blades at the window. "Look!"

Could her friend be any more rude? "I'm not dres—" Everly's heart shot into her throat as her mind registered why her friend showed her the window. Before dawn. Because they'd never see dawn. Snow covered nearly half the window. "No!" she gasped and rushed to the window, touching the icy pane as if that would make it go away. "No no no no. You can't do this to me."

She rushed out of the room and sprinted down the hall, spotting a light coming from Mr. Daily's office. Everly swung herself inside with all her panic. "Mister—" She hauled herself up straight, a chest right in her face. She stumbled back "S–sorry." But then she saw the face. And felt the color and courage leach from her. The man, the guard. She stepped back. Plastered herself against the door as he shoved out, his expression one of barely restrained rage.

"He's angry and just gave me an earful over nothing I have control over, so don't you go doing it, too," Mr. Dailey said. "We couldn't have known what Mother Nature would do while we slept like good humans."

"Mr. Dailey—we're snowed in!"

"Really?" he slammed down the phone in his hand. "I hadn't noticed."

Everly started at his harshness.

Mr. Dailey wilted. "I'm sorry, Miss Sinclair." His brows tangled in his own frustration. "Being here in the lodge for Christmas isn't anything any of us wanted."

"*Christmas?*" Everly breathed. "Are you kidding me?"

He pointed to the windows. "It's nearly six feet and coming down hard still."

"I know," she said with a gulp. "But Christmas!"

"It's not my idea of a good Christmas either, but even if we get a path shoveled, my plow would take a day at least just to clear the parking lot. And county plows won't come up the mountain until the snow slows a lot more because it's just too dangerous on the roads up here." He gave her an apologetic-annoyed look. "We have enough supplies to get you through, but let's just pray we don't lose power. It gets mighty cold up here when that happens."

"Bind your tongue, Mr. Dailey. That's about like jinxing us." Though she'd intended to tease him, Everly had no humor in her words. It'd fled into the drifts barricading them.

"The storm isn't letting up," he said, indicating to the radio. "They're predicting it'll get worse before it gets better."

Everly let out a whimper-growl. "Tonight's the gala."

"We should plan to go on. Might not have troubles with power."

She gave him a wry smile. "If you believed that, I might." Everly deflated. Could this launch fail in any other way?

Right. Just jinx yourself!

She ran a hand through her tangly hair, expelling a long breath. Guess she got to be the bearer of bad news. "What preparations can we undertake while we still have power?"

She touched his shoulder. "Thank you. And," she shuddered a

sigh, feeling the chill of the temperatures through her pajamas, "I'm sorry."

Mr. Dailey shrugged. "It comes with owning a lodge. We have generators, so we'll hope for the best."

"You hope, I'll pray." She left the office and walked a few paces before the grief and fear caught up with her. She trudged out to the foyer and spotted Maren by the large fireplace. Everly went and held out her hands to the flames, then hugged herself.

"What do we do?"

Closed her eyes. Prayed . . . or tried. Harden was working against her. They were now snowed in, which would anger the guests. Which would reflect poorly on Stone.

Would this cost him a solid launch?

No. She wasn't going to let that happen. "Go on."

Maren's brown eyes widened. "Seriously?"

Everly turned and slumped onto the stone ledge, the heat and crackle of the fire at her back. "What else can we do? We can't control the weather. Plows won't be up for a couple of days. We have power, so we go on as planned."

"Wow," Maren said, easing down beside her. "Okay, then."

Something hit her shoulder, but she brushed off what it was, glancing up and glad it wasn't a spark from the fire. Which would be the perfect end to this—to go up in flames. She fingered her pajamas, recalling something about most PJs being fire rated. Were these?

Which was stupid to worry about.

She bent forward and propped the heel of her hands against her forehead. "Everything is going wrong."

"No, it's not. But you are having challenges," Maren said. "And what's that thing you're always saying your Grandpa told you?"

She groaned. "I don't want to be encouraged right now."

"Cheater. But I know it's something about being fierce. And that's you, Everly Sinclair." Maren laughed. "Go get showered and dress, then some coffee."

Straightening did little to help her shed the weight on her shoulders. "I think I need coffee first," Everly countered.

"Well, I need a shower and steam my gown for tonight." Her friend started away.

Another rock hit, this time on her crown. Everly cringed, and looked up, her mind winging to Azzan on the beams two nights ago. This time, however, the rafters were empty. "Hey," she called to Maren, "start thinking up things to get ready if we lose power. Maybe some activities for the kids and the adults."

"Roger, roger," Maren said with a mock salute.

Everly shifted over and put her back against the warmed stone of the fireplace. Stretched out her legs and wanted to pretend none of this was happening. But that wouldn't get her anywhere.

Grandpa, I could really use your help . . .

Or maybe Azzan could help her.

Why she had that idea, she didn't have a clue. He wasn't even talking to her now, for whatever contrived reason. Which was fine. Because she had this launch to save.

Sleep was highly overrated, especially when a person suspected he slept under the same roof as a notorious assassin. What was Peterson doing with this guy? Azzan spent the night, trying to research Åkesson, but he was a guy not readily found on Google or Spies-R-Us searches. Even with Azzan's sophisticated tech, he wasn't getting anywhere. What was going on? He lifted his phone and dialed, hoping for more help this time.

"You're not going to do that lame line on me, again, are you?" Houston asked through the crackling connection.

Azzan snorted. "I'll give you a break this time. Got something I would like your help with."

"By your distraction and tone, this sounds juicy," Houston said.

No wonder the guy had the job he did. He read people about as well as Azzan. "I have a name I need you to research . . ." Maybe he should give Houston some warning, tell him what he could be unleashing if he went full throttle, which is exactly what he needed him to do.

"And I am waiting for that name."

Yeah, he had to prepare this guy. "Houston, this name . . . the trouble that could hit you . . ."

"Yeah, yeah. I got it, but some people—they end up six feet under? Well, I'm twenty." He sniggered, most likely referencing the belowground bunker he worked at in a secure location. "So cough it up, spy-boy. I've got codes to run."

"Melker Åkesson."

"Say again?"

"Melker Åkesson." He spelled the name. "Let me know what you find. And hurry—there's a storm here and we could lose connectivity and power."

"Gotcha."

THE DIRECT APPROACH is the best approach. Grandpa was right again! Everly shared the daunting news directly and succinctly with the guests. Apologized and promised they were doing everything possible to make sure nobody was stranded at Bexar-Wolfe for Christmas. The afternoon's country fair activities were modified and set up inside, and tonight's gala and formal dinner would go forward as planned.

She stood at the back of the smaller ballroom where she, Maren, and Ross had created as much of a "Country Fair" atmosphere as possible. Thankfully, most of the hay bales and props had come in yesterday. Had they not done some pre-work, there would be no hay. But the pony was still in the barn. No way to get the sweet animal over for the fair, thanks to Mother Nature dumping her apron of snow on the mountain. But they did have target practice with a child's crossbow, bobbing for apples, ring toss, and pin-the-tail.

"How're you holding up?" Willow Metcalfe asked as she joined them, wearing a long skirt, sweater, and leather belt that draped from her waist to her hip on the other side.

"Cannot believe we're snowed in. I'm alive. Determined to make this whole thing work."

"I think you're doing a brilliant job, with what's happened."

Everly nodded to the empty pony stall. "A little dull, but not completely ruined."

"Well, the kids are having fun, and the moms are grateful."

"Let's just hope the same can be said for the movers and shakers at tonight's gala." Everly headed toward the door, but then slowed, paused. Realized the woman with her might have answers. "I . . . you know Azzan, right?"

Willow shrugged. "As much as that man can be known."

What a curious thing to say. "What do you mean?"

Folding long thin arms over her chest as they strolled the 'fair grounds,' Willow bunched her shoulders and pursed her lips. "Azzan's pretty secretive. I've known him for more than a half-dozen years and besides the fact he's wicked-quiet and crazy-perceptive, I know that his parents are dead. Piper's his cousin. And . . . he was in the military." She bobbed her head from side to side. "Obviously, if he's working with my brother's team."

"Military." Everly supposed she should've seen that coming, but he didn't really have the edge the way Max and the others did. Well, he did—but it was different.

But his parents were dead. And Piper was his cousin.

"Why?" Willow asked, squatting and reaching out to a blonde three- or four-year-old girl who came barreling into her arms. She lifted and kissed the little one's cheeks.

Envying the family, the laughter, the camaraderie among Canyon's team and its members, Everly felt her throat tighten. Her parents weren't dead, but they also weren't close. She'd spent more time with a nanny then at boarding schools . . . until Grandpa let her live with him in her later teen years.

Willow turned to her. "You okay? Did something happen between you two?"

"*Between us?*" Everly hated the way her voice pitched. She forced a laugh, but it fell short of humor. She had no idea what was between them, except a brick wall.

"You said two words, but your eyes told an entire story," Willow noted. "I'm safe haven here, if you want to talk."

Insane. She didn't even know this woman but could feel her self-imposed dam against spilling her life story cracking. "I guess . . . I told him something pretty . . . personal to me, and . . ."

"He hasn't talked to you since."

Everly nodded.

"Typical male." She lowered the child back to the floor, freeing her to escape off to another adventure. "But Azzan . . . I think personal stuff scares him. It requires a response, a commitment of empathy. I'm not sure he's capable of that."

Surprise turned her toward the elegant-Bohemian woman. "What—"

"Maybe that's not fair," Willow said. "I think to him, knowing private matters requires a commitment from him. And honestly? Other than to the men he thinks of like brothers, I'm not sure Azzan has ever done that."

"I don't understand. What . . . why?" Everly struggled to grasp what that meant. "That's basically just friendship, right? A friend confides, you hold their confidence."

"Again," Willow said with a soft lift of her shoulders, "I'm not even sure Azzan has had that. He's intense, but he's also intensely private. If you want to know more than that, I'd try Piper. Because I'm pretty sure, no matter how much you make him curious, Azzan won't cross his self-imposed lines."

"So, you're telling me to give up."

Willow arched an eyebrow at her. "Give up? I thought there was nothing between you two?" She laughed. "I'm sorry. That wasn't fair either." The expression she threw at Everly should've made her defensive or annoyed, but instead it only came across as empathetic. "It's so obvious you like him. And I don't blame you."

"I'm well aware of how he knocks my thoughts and heart sideways, but . . ."

"Does he like you back?"

Everly felt the heat climbing into her cheeks. "Every time I think he does, there's this arctic wind that blows across everything. We were talking on the mountain, now—silence. Oh, and when he got attacked, I helped clean up the scratches. Then he nearly kissed me, now—all quiet."

Willow froze. Dropped her gaze, then met Everly's, lifting both eyebrows nearly into her hairline. "Nearly kissed you?"

"Once." She'd never forget it either. And that's what drove her mad—it was all she could think of, the lost kiss. Stolen was more like it—because he started to give it to her then took it back.

"He and I dated—*one time.* But he was too intense, and for him,

I was too open for him."

"Open?"

Willow smiled as she glided toward another child. "I'm an open book he wasn't willing to read."

IN HIS SUITE getting ready for the gala, Azzan stuffed his arms into the dress shirt and heard his phone. Working the buttons, he moved to the dresser and eyed the screen. He snatched it. "Houston?"

"Yeah, *now* we have a problem."

"What kind of problem?" His mind whiplashed through a dozen possible scenarios, including Houston being hauled in for accessing Above Top Secret intel.

"You're not going to believe this."

Checking his watch, he knew he'd catch flak from the guys if he was late. They all knew he hated gigs like this, but he owed it to Everly to be on time and on top of security. He grabbed his dress jacket, skipping a tie altogether.

"He's got diplomatic immunity because he's working with Senator Peterson."

Stopped cold by those words and the icy blast from the past, Azzan stared at the door. "Bull! He's a freakin' assassin!"

"Working with Senator Peterson on some . . . something or the other that's way above my pay grade." Clacking of keys and creaking chairs droned in the background. "And yeah, I'm not digging anymore because I do like living, and I do like keeping my job. I've got Boone and Trace breathing down my neck for disrupting their perfectly ordered world."

He had no idea who those people were, but it didn't matter. "I need intel on this guy, Houston." He slipped the gun into the holster strapped around his waist. "I need to know what he looks like. Where he's been. What's he—"

"I can help with the first one but not the rest. In fact . . ." His fingers zipped and zapped, then he grunted. "And there it is in your inbox."

Azzan's phone buzzed.

"Merry Christmas. And don't call me again." Houston hung up.

With a groan and massage of his forehead, Azzan dropped against the bed. Opened the file Houston had sent and found himself staring back at Peterson's thug. He hung his head, pinching the bridge of his nose. It was him. Melker Åkesson was here. He could feel the tendrils of his past coming loose, threatening to drown him. Threatening to take him down.

Head cradled in his hands, he closed his eyes. Willed the torrent of rage to die down. He hadn't allowed that side of him dominance in years. He couldn't do it again. Wouldn't. It hadn't resolved anything then. It wouldn't now.

But he was here. He would pursue and threaten and push and attack until there was nothing left of Azzan. Nothing left breathing.

Åkesson just didn't know the assassin he hunted was dead and buried.

Had to be.

He wouldn't let this nightmare unleash and harm innocents, hurt Everly.

Why? Why now? Why did he have to show up when Azzan found someone worth chasing? Love worth risking?

You don't even know her!

But he did. Might not have known every trace of her past, but he knew the woman Everly Sinclair . . .

LeMarque.

Kind of stupid falling for America's Granddaughter, America's Sweetheart. That's what the press had called her. The sweet kid who'd endured being raised in the limelight with her grandfather, often propped on his knee during the early years in office. Surviving the attack that stole her grandfather and her innocence.

And what would Azzan Yasir bring?

Heartache. Confusion. Trouble. Danger. More death.

"Well."

Jerking straight, knife snatched from its sheath before he even met her eyes, Azzan stared down Willow. "What are you doing here?"

"Down, grizzly," she said in that taunting voice of hers. "I knocked—lightly"—she said with a bob of her head—"but still a knock. Your door slipped open."

Had he been that careless?

Yes. He'd been heading out when Houston dropped the truth bomb. "What do you want?" he growled.

"To smack your thick skull, that's what!"

He glowered at her. "I have—"

"To be very careful."

Azzan stilled, sensing in her words what he knew needed to be said. "Don't worry. I know—she's off-limits. Canyon already told me."

"Actually, I came here to tell you she's crazy about you." Willow folded her arms. "Which presents an interesting problem."

He jammed his gaze to the side, not quite looking at her. "No problem. Not from her. But we do have another one. And I need you to stay with her."

"You're really crazy about her, aren't you?"

He ignored her words. Ignored the way they'd clogged his veins with dread. With excitement. No, dread. "I believe there's a credible threat against me—Peterson's guard. If he . . ." He ground his molars, unable to say what struggled violently through his heart.

"I understand, but, Azzan. She cares, likes y—"

"I don't care! *Nobody* else is dying because of me."

CHAPTER 13

B ALLOON ARCHES HAD been replaced with simple, elegant evergreen swags and red plaid bows. A tree glittered happily in the corner of the grand ballroom, drawing the eye from the two-dozen round tables lined with red tablecloths and adorned with rustic centerpieces of wood blocks, evergreen sprigs, silver ornaments and candles.

At the front of the room, four tables were put end-to-end and decorated as the other tables. In the middle, a lectern in the middle. A banner adorned with Stone's emblem draped it. The band and Hugh Coton were setting up for a lively, entertaining event.

And in the middle of the room, she found Stone talking with his brothers, Colton, and Griffin. And Azzan. Even though Stone wasn't facing her, his consternation screamed across the room.

Apparently, more than the decorations had changed.

Her stomach squeezed then writhed as she forced herself through the tables. When her heel hit the dance floor, the men turned. While she sensed appreciative smiles and looks from the group, it was the brilliance of Azzan's non-smile that vaulted her lunch up her throat.

Blowing out a slow, long breath, she joined them. Accepted compliments. But turned her gaze to Stone deliberately.

He brandished a broad smile. "You look beautiful."

Touching her nape, where a few loose strands tickled, Everly shook her head. "Thank you. But is everything okay?" She glanced to the men, who were drifting away, Azzan lingering closer than the others.

"A few security concerns," he said quietly.

Her gaze turned to Azzan, but he was staring away. Intentionally not looking at her. Ignoring her. "Really? I wasn't informed of any—"

"It's more than that," Stone said, his voice a knot of frustration and concern. "Peterson's not convinced I'm running on the right platform. He wants me to use education and health-care reform."

Everly groaned. "Everyone's doing that. And nobody's winning. They're like piranhas feeding off each other on the Hill."

"But they are real problems for real people, average people. Like me." He seemed to be uncapping a vial of poison and dumping it into their cocktails tonight.

Everly nodded, feeling the shifting sand on which she stood. Fighting the urge to curl her freshly manicured hands around Harden's neck, she dared not breathe his name. "This sounds . . . like someone's whispers in your ear." She lifted her chin. "That's not what you're about, Stone. It's why I offered to do this. It's why I asked to run your campaign. I believe in you and what you're about. Nobody wants the same ol' same ol'."

"But same ol' is what they know, and people are creatures of habit," Stone said, feeding the panic pill to her again. "They want what's familiar. Get too far out of that and—"

"Are you backing out?" Blurting out the question might make her look weak, but desperation forced a girl to do dumb things.

Stone twitched. "No." He huffed. "I'm just . . . concerned."

"It's a risk. We knew that."

Laughter carried into the room as the guests started arriving.

Everly had to turn this conversation and her own courage back toward something positive. "Personally, I think things are going well." She nodded. "We'll serve the meal, then I'll introduce you, and you'll give your grand pronouncement. Afterward, I'll close out the evening for dancing and merriment."

When Stone joined the guests flooding the room, welcoming them, working to build a sense of merriment he clearly didn't feel, Everly rubbed the back of her neck.

It seemed this entire weekend was set against her! After placing her purse in the chair at her place, she forced herself to follow Stone's example. Throwing herself into the evening, into talking politics, convincing people Stone was on top of things, that he could do this, she forgot about her own insecurities.

"You are a brave soul, Miss Sinclair," a nasally voice said.

Steeling her spine, Everly turned to Senator Peterson. "Why? Because I sat you next to Blanche Woodside?" she taunted him, referencing one of the most influential lobbyists on the Hill.

He sniffed and nearly rolled his eyes. Rude. "Are you sure about Metcalfe?"

Only then did she note the simpering idiot behind the senator. "Senator, you know full well who my family is, and you know well how seriously I take that, especially since my grandfather's murder by a coward who lurked in the shadows." She slid her gaze to Harden again.

A bell chimed as Maren adjusted the microphone noisily—and on purpose. "Ladies and gentlemen, if you'd be so kind as to please take your seats so the staff can begin serving."

Everly made her way to the head table and planted herself at the end of the table, leaving the prime spots for Stone and his mother, at his insistence. Steaks and potatoes were served, quickly devoured, then replaced with decadent tiramisu cheesecake and crème brûlée. Of course, with nerves plaguing her, Everly didn't trust herself to eat and not end up either vomiting or wearing the food. So, she tucked chunks of dinner rolls into her mouth, and waited.

Watching the clock tick down proved as painful as noting how Azzan sat chatting casually with a young woman—some senator's younger sister—the whole evening. What had she done to make him so angry that he wouldn't talk to her?

"Ev," Ross whispered, nodding to the clock. "Time."

Heart caught in her throat, she lifted her folio and made her way to the lectern, stopping along the way at Stone. "Ready?" she whispered, leaning down.

"As ever," he said with a look to his mom, then Everly.

At the lectern, Everly placed her speech on the sloped surface, adjusted the microphone with a meaty grate through the sound system, then began. "Good evening. Wasn't that a wonderful meal and dessert? Thank you, Bexar-Wolfe Lodge for wonderful food and service the last few days." She stepped back and applauded, drawing the rest of the audience into the same. "I'd like to thank each of our sitting congress-persons and representatives for attending this event.

Please stand," she said, ending by recognizing each politician by name. "Tonight, you are all here to give witness and support to the hope of a bright new future for our great state. When I first approached then-Sheriff Metcalfe about running for office, I ended up in jail."

Laughter rippled through the room. "He said it was only a tour, but I'm not convinced." More laughter, settling Everly into her introductory speech, which brought Stone to the microphone a few minutes later. His conviction-laced speech was dotted with humor and intelligence. It reminded Everly why she'd so ardently supported this man. Why she believed he could make it to the governor's mansion.

"This, ladies and gentlemen, friends, loved ones," Stone said firmly as he glanced around the room—and it seemed he was struggling against tears—"is why I'm doing this. To honor what my father said, 'If you want something changed, do it yourself.' Oh." Stone straightened. Glanced at his mom. "I think my mom said that . . . every time a job was left undone."

Again, laughter swept the room as Stone bent down and kissed his mom's cheek. A great moment, captured by the photographer on hand. "But this is why, friends—this is why I am officially announcing my candidacy for governor!"

Applause erupted for several long minutes as Stone stood there, a perfect photo op that would be shared with the press. When the clapping finally drew down and Stone resumed his seat beside his mom, Everly took the lectern again, thanking the guests for their continued patience, promised to keep them updated on the weather conditions, then formally introduced Hugh Coton and allowed the music and dancing to fill the rest of the evening.

An hour later, music wafted through the hall and drew the guests to the dance floor. Everly deflated in her seat and prayed she could just relax while others enjoyed themselves. For a moment, she grieved that Grandpa wasn't here, that he couldn't see this moment. She was sure he would celebrate her victory and congratulate Stone on what would surely be a promising run to election night. But as she thought of him, as she longed to share this time, she knew she couldn't. And grief became suffocating.

Everly pushed out a side door and found solace in the cooler, quieter corner of the grand foyer. The stone patio had been cleared of snow but still sat barricaded by a wall of snow. Though she hadn't brought a shawl or coat, she slipped outside. Inhaled the crisp air, then let a few tears fall.

He would've been so proud. She was sure. Not because it was her. But because of Stone. "Oh Grandpa," she whispered, heat pluming around her words.

Though shivers turned into violent tremors, she refused to return to the noise and chaos of the dancing, the throbbing music reaching her even here. She looked up at the sky, thick with clouds and falling snow. She should feel trapped, but she only felt free. Exhilarated.

Her teeth clacked hard, the shiver tearing through her body.

Warmth draped her shoulders and nearly bare back.

Everly started, reaching to where boiled wool covered her, and found Azzan at her side. "I . . . thanks."

WARRING WITHIN HER, she seemed ready to toss his jacket on the snowy ground or throw herself into his arms.

He hoped for the latter, but he had no right.

Azzan slid his hands into the pockets of his slacks, and stared up over the snow bank that had been driven back with metal and brute force. Much as he'd driven back his feelings for her. He had to talk to her. But how did one exactly tell the most beautiful, intelligent woman that he killed for a living?

She turned toward the doors, whispering, "I should go inside."

Irritated with himself, frantic at losing the chance to tell her, he caught her arm. "Wait." He turned to her. Saw the jacket slipping from her bare shoulder and slid it back on, feeling a warm zap through his fingertips when he grazed her clavicle.

She hesitated, her gaze and head down. Wary. Scared.

He hated that. Hated her being afraid of him. And what would she be when she found out the truth. When he told her, because that's why he had come out here to think, never imagining she'd come out too, with her bare shoulders and hair done up.

He took her chin and tipped it up, forcing her gaze to his. The jacket again slipped, and this time, he threaded her hand through the sleeves. She managed a nervous smile, then brought her gaze to his again.

He traced the gentle arc of her face and jaw. Brushed the back of his hand over her cheek. Inched closer at the brightening that washed through her face, her eyes, her cheeks. Her lips, which parted as he slid his fingers around her neck. Drew her closer.

Everly took in a breath, tense in anticipation, but clearly wanting this as much as he did.

Stand off.

Her palms, resting on his arms after he had somehow caught her waist, slid up his arms, igniting a fire he could not control. One he did not want to.

Azzan bent in and took the kiss he'd ached for these many weeks. Tested her. Eyed her, enjoying the fluttering of her breath and eyelashes. He caught her lips again, lingering. Feeling the pull of the tide between them. Knowing he was sinking fast.

You'll get her—

Her hands in his hair unseated any reserve he had left.

Greedily, he hooked an arm around her waist and hauled her into his arms. Crushed her against his chest. Captured her mouth fully. Kissed her. Deep. Long. Fingers pressing her shoulder blades in. Feeling her sweet moan against his chest.

Everly's locked her arms around his neck and clung to him, trembling.

Shivering. Cold.

He turned away from the snowy balustrade. Everly stumbled, but steadied herself as he caught her between himself the lodge wall. He kissed her again. And again. Traced the line of her jaw. The soft spot beneath her ear, which made her pull in a quick, shocked breath, as he moved down her neck to the hollow of her throat.

He felt her tense, moan, then he pressed his lips to hers once more. Deepened it. Wished for more. Wanted more.

Crack!

Screams and gunfire strafed the night.

CHAPTER 14

AZZAN STAGGERED TO a stop, breaking the kiss. Pressed a hand to the wall to catch his bearings. Mind ricocheting from pure elation to alarm as he came to grips with what his tactical brain barked to his carnal mind—gunfire!

Everly trembled in his arms, her face flushed, hair disheveled as her wide, beautiful eyes came to his. He had a feeling if he hadn't pinned her against the wall, she'd have collapsed with fright. "Wh–what was that?"

Adrenaline hijacked his passion.

He cursed himself. Cursed his weakness. Cursed this whole blasted night! "Stay here," he said, hauling himself together.

Everly grabbed onto him, panicked. "N–no." She was trembling again, but this time for a very different reason. "Don't leave me. Please." Terror streaked through her blush-filled face. He saw in her eyes the memory of watching her grandfather murdered. Of the fall that nearly killed her. And he knew—*knew* he could not leave her.

So . . . options?

Gaze hitting the interior of the lodge, seeing people spilling out of the ballroom, then armed men in tactical gear terrorizing them back under control, Azzan worked scenarios. Whoever had hit the lodge—was there really any question when Åkesson was here?— wanted hostages. Wanted to control the people, herding them back into the ballroom under threat of being shot.

Azzan cursed. Why hadn't he just told Everly about Åkesson, about himself?

"What?" She twisted around just in time to see two men headed their way.

Disentangling himself from her, Azzan stepped back. Scanned

the terrace. Snow. Balustrade. A bit of height and more snow. Balcony. Good, good. But . . . Everly couldn't do the moves he could.

Leave her. Gain the vantage. Stay free to protect—

"Azzan?" Her voice drowned in fear as her fingers grazed his arm.

Obeying his instincts, he hopped and grabbed the ledge of the balcony.

"No!" Everly shriek-groaned, catching his sleeve.

The touch knocked him off balance, frigid snow biting into his fingers as he held his grip. Firmed his balance. Then—

Door punched open.

Amid Everly's scream, Azzan flipped himself up onto the balcony. Eyes closed, he stayed. Better chance to stop this if he got away. But if they hurt her because of him . . .

Go! She'll only live if you—

"Come down, Azzan," came a greasy voice, "or I have orders to kill her. Right here."

In a squat on the balcony, Azzan hung his head. Wiped a hand over his mouth. Cursed himself for the thousandth time for caving to his feelings for her. It was stupid. A mistake.

Get out of here. She has a better chance to survive if you stay alive.

"Or should I taste what you've tasted?"

There came the sound of shuffled feet. A meaty impact—stone on brick. Everly's yelp and whimper. She cried out, objecting.

His mind played havoc with what was happening, how the piece of crap probably had her pinned to the wall. Violating her.

Fury had him toeing the rail in a fluid, effortless move. Leapt into the air, twisting as he did, so he again faced the lodge, then caught the rail. Shots peppered the night as he swung his legs down like a ramming beam, straight into the man pinning Everly to the wall.

The man's head hit the wall. He stumbled.

Azzan landed. Threw a hard right hook. Nailed the guy in the face. Following the momentum that landed the guy against the wall, Azzan pounded his head into the ground. A weight plowed into him, but he merely stumbled. Then jumped up and spun around, aiming a left reverse hook kick at the new attacker.

But a sight warned him of the mistake.

The man held a gun to Everly's head.

Azzan snapped in his leg. Landed in a crouch, then slowly rose, trying to ignore the tears streaking down Everly's face. Trying to ignore her gut-wrenching sobs. "We both know I can end you before you pull that trigger." It wasn't true. The chances were fifty-fifty, if that good. And it wasn't a risk he'd take.

"Inside," the man growled.

"Give her to me first," Azzan said, his words those of warning.

The man hesitated, then pitched her forward.

Azzan caught her. And though Everly's hands clutched at him, he swirled her behind him. Out of direct line of sight.

The man held an M4 at them. "Inside."

Sidestepping as he guided Everly, Azzan kept his gaze on the gunman. Though he considered shoving her inside and coldcocking the gunman, Azzan remembered the firepower inside. Guns ready to level opposition. It'd be a lost cause. Besides, even if he could neutralize the guard, Everly would have to get free. Run. But to where? The Lodge was snowed in.

So, they had to stay alive. Find out what was going on. Find a way out.

Shoved into the ballroom, Azzan stepped back, his instincts flying, his anger ruling. But he heard Everly's gasp. Saw the frightened faces in the room. And stymied his response. The greedy gleam in the man's eyes warned him they'd love for him to remove himself from this equation.

"*Leave him!*" a voice thundered, then more quietly ordered, "Bring him—bring them both right here."

Azzan met the odious eyes of Melker Åkesson. Amid cowering, kneeling guests, he waited in the center of the dance floor.

Dread spilled through Azzan. He had the guests grouped close to lessen the chance they'd leave alive. That one or two could slip out, be a source of frustration and—

"Miss LeMarque, have you any idea who the man is that you were lip-locked with on the terrace?"

Azzan balled his fists, glowering at the man who'd defeated him once. Who'd outplayed and outsmarted him. The dark thought struck Azzan that if he'd been able to finish this when he and

Åkesson last met, the assassin wouldn't have killed Everly's grandpa. Did that mean Azzan must shoulder that blame, too? What would she say?

"A man ten times better than you," Everly gritted out as they forced her onto the hard floor.

Åkesson barked a laugh. "Delicious." He clapped, entirely too pleased with himself.

As Azzan led the way to the dance floor, he saw the body splayed out on the floor. Senator Peterson. So much for Metcalfe's backing from the senator. He tried to shield Everly from the gruesome sight.

"Oh no. No, no, no," Åkesson crooned. "I want her to see this, understand what's at stake, what I am willing to do."

A guard yanked Everly from his protection and shoved her nearly into the pool of blood around Peterson's head like a sick halo.

Everly yelped and threw herself back, shielding her face.

"This is between you and me," Azzan bit out. "Let them——"

Another barked laugh. "You were never very good at figuring things out, Azzan. That was your fatal flaw. It's how I nearly carved out your eye. How I beat you into submission once, and I will do it again!"

"What do you want? Why now?" Fury. Rage. Need to kill. They surged and roiled through Azzan's veins. Instincts he'd long suppressed came roaring back.

Then panic. He didn't want Everly to hear this. Didn't want her to know. . . *God, help me!* He didn't want her to know the truth of him. Didn't want to see that remonstration in her beautiful eyes.

Åkesson grabbed Everly by the hair, dragging her up. He pulled her against himself, arm hooked around her throat. Gun aimed at Azzan. "Do you see him, fair Everly?"

Azzan shook his head. "Åkesson."

Another annoying laugh. "You figured it out. Well done, Azzan." He pressed his cheek to Everly's. "He's handsome, isn't he?"

Tears streaked down her face as she held her attacker's arm to avoid being choked.

"You like him—a lot. Don't you?" He was taunting her. Getting her to admit what she felt for Azzan, not to force a confession, but to wound her deeper. "Handsome man. Green eyes. Raw. Intense. Exactly what the ladies like." He looked at her, still smashing their cheeks together. "Do you love him, little Everly?"

She whimpered, gaze pleading, begging Azzan to intervene. But how did he do that without hurting her? He gave her a small shake of his head. Tried to warn her.

Åkesson hauled her up harder. Choked her.

Everly cried out, the sound of breath struggling through her throat shoving Azzan forward.

Men fell on him, slamming him back to the ground. "I swear, Åkesson—if you hurt her—"

"You mean like an assassin hurt your mother?"

Azzan stilled. Lifted hooded, angry eyes to the assassin, simultaneously noting the wives of Nightshade shifting positions. Slipping back. The team was closing the gap.

Pressing the muzzle to her temple again, Åkesson drew her backward a couple of feet, having discerned that Azzan had gained ground. Gotten closer.

"Tell me, Everly, is it love that makes you cry for the man on the floor."

"We barely know each other," Azzan hissed.

"By the way you were eating her face, Azzan, I don't think I'd agree. What of all those texts you sent her?"

How did he know that? Molten dread poured into Azzan's gut. "Why?" he demanded. "Why now? How'd you find me?"

A nauseating laugh emanated from the man. "Now tell me, Everly," Åkesson said, shifting the aim of the weapon to Azzan. "Do you love this man?"

Something shifted in her expression. The panic and fright sheared off beneath the man's question.

Oh no.

Everly blinked away the tears. Hardened her expression. "Yes," she gritted out.

"Good, good," Åkesson said.

"What do you care?" Azzan demanded. "Leave her—"

"Leave her? Oh, I intend to leave her all right—dead, on a cold slab."

"If you want to harm me, then harm *me*. I'm sick of your

game—"

Åkesson shot him a look of confusion, then amusement. "You think this is about you?" A mocking laugh wafted through the thick tension of the room.

"Then what? Why now?"

Confusion weighted Azzan. Stifled his response. His mind catching up with this whole scenario. The effort that went into it. The man's diplomatic immunity, long in place before this event. This wasn't about Stone or Peterson or even Azzan.

Oh crap. No. No no no.

"He knocked me over the bannister . . ."

Falling petals.

A coward. An assassin.

He had it wrong. He had it all wrong. "You," he growled. "You killed her grandfather."

"And I'd thought I'd cleaned up behind myself, but the little imp had an iron spine, apparently."

Everly went rigid. Eyes flung wide as panic seized her, hauling a ragged, wheezing breath through her lungs.

"More like an iron will," Azzan growled. He wouldn't let this happen. Wasn't going to let someone rip a woman he loved from his arms again. "Why? Why now? Why here?"

"Because—it's poetic. When I found out she was alive, I came. But then . . . the terrific justice that you were trying to seduce America's Granddaughter. Two birds with one Stone."

The weapon snapped to his face, and only then did Azzan realize he had come to his feet. And though he'd been so thoroughly focused on Åkesson and Everly's cries and the panic that nearly drove him to a mistake, Azzan saw it now. It wouldn't end like this. He wouldn't let it.

"Down!" Åkesson hissed. "Down, or I end—"

A calmness not his own descended. Blanketed his shoulders. Told him to stand firm. Stand for those who could not stand for themselves. Deliberately, he angled to the side, giving the assassin less surface to hit with any bullets. "No."

"*Down!*" Outrage blinded the man to the movement of those around him. To Nightshade, crawling into position like the deadly operators they were, neutralizing guards, one by one. The crowds shifted away silently.

Azzan turned Everly, who was so riddled with confusion. Fear. She saw the truth of this situation. Of what and who he was. Though her gaze was locked onto him, he was not convinced— would not believe—she saw anything but an animal. A coward.

"Tell her what you are!"

Still locked in her gaze, Azzan tried to telegraph reassurance. Tried to relay instructions. To be still. To be quiet. But he saw it. Saw the hurt. The anguish.

"She knows what I am," Azzan said, owning the truth. Hating every bitter cell of it. Of himself.

"No," she whimpered, tears puddling in her eyes. Making her gold eyes look like pools of melted honey. "No."

"Everly." He spoke calmly, firmly, lifting a hand.

"See, *sweet Evvy*, your hero isn't a hero."

Everly's eyes went wide. White.

The nickname. The name her Grandpa called her.

Boom! Snap! Crack!

Darkness dropped on the lodge.

Azzan seized the distraction. Dove at Åkesson.

Gunfire seared the air.

CHAPTER 15

IN THE SEA of black, Everly felt herself falling backwards. She screamed, feeling the weightlessness. The tease of falling petals in the air. The stranglehold of terror. The void that roared and devoured. The crack of her back on the marble floor.

Grandpa.

The face. That face. *His* face!

Her head bounced, thudding hard twice. Jolting her from black to white. Night and day. She screamed. Tears streamed from her eyes into her ears.

She didn't care. She couldn't move.

Hands pawed at her.

She cried out.

"Everly!"

She blinked, only seeing a bloody face above her. No petals. No marble floor.

"Everly!"

"Maren?"

Hands gripped her arms. Shoulders. Pulled her aside.

Sliding away from the chaos, away from Azzan and that man, Everly dragged her mind from the nightmare. From the past. Found herself wading in a thick darkness and panic of the present—of that man who'd—

No. No, it couldn't be.

"Everly. You with us?"

She stared at the face in front of her. Blinked. Blinked again. "Willow."

The woman nodded. Then turned her. "Out. Go."

Through the bleeding darkness of an emergency light that

caressed the strange void that captured the lodge, Everly saw people fast-crawling through a small crack in the divider between rooms.

As she hurried behind the exodus, she realized the darkness was a power outage. It'd taken her too long to figure that out. Too long to think of—"Azzan."

She peered over her shoulder and saw a tangle of bodies. Saw the fury of Azzan's expression. Out on the terrace, she'd seen that there too. Seen a side of him she'd neither anticipated nor wanted.

Someone shoved her backside with a terse "move!"

Scrabbling through the opening, she found herself in the smaller ballroom. Hands pulled her up. Ross and Range pitched her toward another door. Following the trail of guests, she hated herself for leaving Azzan.

Then hated herself for caring.

He's an assassin.

The thought slowed her. Made her legs sluggish. Heart staggering, she stared at the door. At the people fleeing. At the insanity. The fear. The panic. The . . . She glanced back to the opening.

Azzan.

Petals falling.

Screams. The man who held her. Choked her. Threatened Azzan. Demanded she say she loved him.

Azzan.

Who was he? How could she . . . how could he . . .?

A wall of bodies swarmed toward her, carrying her out of the room. Away from the danger. To safety.

Azzan threw himself at the danger. At the assassin.

Azzan's an assassin.

An assassin.

He kills people.

Like the coward who killed Grandpa.

Her mind fractured. She cried. Curled into a ball.

Peripherally aware as they huddled into a room with children. Doors locked. A petite blond woman trained a weapon on the door. Range and Ross were protecting the other door. Mothers huddled with children, whispering songs, whispering promises of safety.

But there was no safety.

It was an illusion.

Azzan was an illusion.

Shots echoed through the dark lodge. Shouts.

Everly glanced to the door. Wondered . . . wondered about Azzan.

He's an assassin.

A coward.

Like the one who killed Grandpa.

Petals falling.

Darkness.

Broken back.

No. No, not like Azzan.

Yes, just like Azzan.

A killer.

He threw himself at that other man.

Feral. Feral was how she could describe his expression when Åkesson grabbed her. Something went absolutely wild and primal in Azzan's expression.

Because Åkesson threatened me.

No, because Åkesson exposed Azzan.

"So help me, if you don't answer me, I'm going to smack you."

Everly blinked. Glanced to the right where Maren sat, a strange splash of light bathing her brown complexion—a glow stick. She held one between them. "Thank God," Maren muttered.

Everly frowned. "What?"

With a huff, Maren sagged against the wall. "I've been sitting here for the last twenty minutes trying to get you to talk to me."

"Why?"

"Because!" Maren's eyes watered. "Because I was afraid you'd lost it. That he'd broken you."

Everly's gaze drifted to the door. *Broken me.* He did that once—Åkesson. Snuffed out Grandpa's life. *Broke my back.* Ended everything good and lovely.

A thought shoved Everly to her feet with a gasp. "No," she breathed, glancing around the room at the children, who knew something was wrong, but tried to listen to the failing reassurances of their mothers.

The petite blond sidled toward her, weapon held toward the

door. "What's wrong?"

"It's me. He doesn't want Azzan. He's after me—Åkesson."

"Good," the woman said, starting back to her position.

"Good?" Everly stomped forward. "He might kill them—"

"Ever held a gun?" The woman extended it to Everly, who cringed. "Ever fired one on a real person? You ready to put lead through that man's skull and live with it every waking second of the rest of your life?"

Everly drew back, startled. Hurt. Powerless. She couldn't just stand here. Not again, not when—

"Easy, Kazi," a soothing voice said. A boy resting against her bosom and snoring, Max's wife met her with a weary gaze.

"No, she needs to get it through her head, if she's with Aladdin—"

"I'm not."

"Then why did the guy nearly kill you over him?"

Sydney Jacobs sighed. "Look, let's just calm down." She faked a smile to Everly. "Kazi is right—the best we can do is protect the children and ourselves. Stay alive."

Looking again to the door, Everly dug through a myriad thoughts. She hated Azzan—for not telling her, for being an assassin, for taking lives. But she didn't hate. No, she did. She should—didn't normal people hate his kind? He was an assassin.

If she's with Aladdin . . . nearly kill you over him . . .

"And the men will do what they do best."

"Which is?" Everly asked.

Kazi smiled. "Neutralize."

"ANYONE GOT EYES on him?" Max's hissed into the darkness.

With his left eye nearly swollen shut, Azzan struggled to have eyes on anything. But as far as he could tell, the only prone figure was Peterson's. The women had fled, then the guests. Unfortunately, the enemy they hadn't taken down escaped out the opposite doors. "Negative." They probably wanted to regroup and rearm. The lodge's loss of power both worked in their favor—

distracting Åkesson long enough for Azzan to attack—and against them, because they were now having to hunt down that animal in the pitch back. Now, he sat here waiting with Canyon, Griffin, and Max. Range, Stone and his guards went to protect the women and children under Max's orders.

But thanks to the lackadaisical quality of Åkesson's team, Nightshade now found itself armed. Not heavily, but hopefully enough to equalize things a little.

Azzan eyed the main doors. "Probably waiting for us."

"Agreed," Max muttered, doing a press check on the handgun he'd lifted. "But we can't stay in here waiting to eat lead."

"Let's find another exit, ladies," Griffin said.

"Roger that," Canyon said, nodding behind them. "Window."

Glancing over his shoulder, Azzan saw the glass cracked by a bullet that had gone rogue when he'd tackled Åkesson. Chaos had erupted, and though he fought like heck to keep the guy down, Åkesson's guys pummeled him. Forced Azzan to release him, then took off running.

"We do that, we are left out in the cold," Griffin reminded them.

"Find another way."

"No other way," Canyon said. "Route the women took and the main doors."

Remembering the gap the smaller ballroom had, the one that allowed him to watch Everly undetected, Azzan's gaze rose to the ceiling.

"Unless you're Superman, that ain't happening," Canyon mumbled.

"Room next to us has an open ceiling." Azzan sprinted toward the long row of tables where the team had been having dinner an hour earlier. He leapt up and used it to springboard himself to the ceiling. He punched and grabbed the support, dangling, feeling the bar give immediately. He flipped the panel out of the way and hoisted himself up into the ceiling. Crouched, head dusting the floor of the second level as he scanned.

"Dude makes it look like riding a bicycle," Canyon muttered.

"Like you and a surfboard," Griffin said, his voice drawing closer.

"Totally different animal."

Azzan spotted it—the opening. "I was right. We can use this to get down the hall."

"And by 'we' you mean this two-hundred-fifty pound—"

"Two-forty," Griffin corrected.

"—oaf."

"I think you mean *oof*," Griffin warned, "as in the sound you're about to make when my fist punches you."

"Azzan," Max said. "Check it out. See if it's clear for us to exfil out the main doors."

"Roger." He scurried in a pattern that took him wide around the entrance to the ballroom. Didn't want to give himself away. When he reached what he felt was a safe spot, he lay across the beams, slowed his breathing, then worked to carefully lift the ceiling panel in the hall. Thank God this was an old place with ceiling tiles rather than the newer integrated ceilings. He peered out and scanned the hall. His gut clenched at the shadows waiting. Peered down the far end on the other side. At least a dozen thugs waiting.

But why so far away? Odd. They had better chances of—

The door! Azzan flinched at the gray brick taped to the door.

He scurried back to the team. "They're out there waiting."

"Then we spray and pray?"

"Negative," Azzan said. "C4 taped to the door."

"Then we're screwed?"

"Negative," he repeated. "But I have an idea."

IT'D BEEN THIRTY MINUTES since the lodge fell silent. Within the child care rooms, the younger children had fallen asleep. Ear buds and games—on a device or phone—kept the older kids quiet and distracted.

"We need a plan," Kazi said. "We're fish in a barrel here if those guys come down this hall."

Canyon's brother nodded as the adults gathered. "Our options are limited, with the snow up to the windows. We can try to dig or somehow melt it. Vents aren't big enough. Ceiling doesn't have tiles like the ballrooms, or that might be worth a try."

"I could go," Kazi suggested. "Slip out, find a route to someplace safe."

"Where is safe?" Piper said. "We are snowed into a lodge. No matter where we go, there's no exit."

As Range and Kazi worked through options, Everly thought of all the little ones, having fun at the fair earlier today. So many innocents, and she could be the cause of their deaths.

Cause of death.

Assassin.

How many people had Azzan killed? How many never saw him coming?

She shivered, realizing his uncanny ability to sneak up on her, to see her when she couldn't see him . . . all because he was an assassin. A deadly person who lived in the shadows.

The shadows of a great hall. Grandpa's home.

Falling petals.

Everly eyed the snow that seemed gray, packed against the windows. It reflected the screens from the devices.

"You love him?"

She twitched and looked up into the same green eyes Azzan had. Piper Neeley was a beautiful woman with blonde hair cut just below her shoulders. Athletic build and serene nature.

Guilt chugged through Everly. She thought she loved him— until she knew what he was. "I . . ." Was she a terrible for person for being unsure now?

"I remember when I first saw Azzan again, after being separated from him for years—and realizing he was Mossad."

Everly started. "Israeli—I thought he was Palestinian?"

"Both," Piper said. "Our grandfather and his mother were Israeli. His father, Palestinian."

Whoa. "That doesn't happen every day."

"It was a forbidden love, his parents'." She nodded, then gave Everly a long, considering look. "What he did for Mossad scares you."

Everly dropped her gaze. "You make that sound bad." Her voice sounded small even to her. "But my grandfather was killed by an assassin as he slept. He nearly killed me." She drew in a heavy breath. "It was the same man from tonight."

"That's why you think he's going to come after you."

She nodded.

"And you think because you met one man who killed, you have met them all."

Everly frowned at her. "Men who kill—"

Piper smiled. "What about women?"

A scowl now tugged at her face.

"I was IDF—Israeli Defense Force. Two years."

"You killed?"

"No," Piper said softly, "but a friend of mine, another woman, she had to kill a man. He had explosives. If she did not kill him, the man would have killed children in a schoolyard."

"Well, that's different."

"Is it?" Piper angled her head. "How?"

"The man was doing harm."

"And you think Azzan only killed innocents like your grandfather?"

Everly swallowed. "I see your point."

"Do you?" Piper smiled sweetly at her. "Because I see a young woman my cousin has taken a great risk over. Threw his anger and his skills at a man who wanted one thing—to kill you."

Boom!

Thud! Thud!

The lodge shook. Dust rained down and a deep rumbling seemed to prowl through the floor.

Range snapped straight. "That was an explosion!" He shoved himself against the door, listened. "Voices distant."

"Open it," Kazi said, lifting the weapon up.

Range nodded then yanked it, leading Kazi out and to the left.

Drawn by the terror of this assassin once more killing someone she loved, Everly was moving without thinking. Heading right, knowing the ins and outs of the lodge via a shortcut past the staff hall, to the main lobby. Somehow, she found herself running. Scared. Of what?

Finding Azzan dead.

She rounded a corner, a haze of smoke and shots skidding her to a halt.

From the ceiling, men dropped, weapons aimed and firing.

Shadows morphed from the corners, firing. Shooting. Two men tripped and fell—no, they were shot!

The haze drifted, snaking around bodies, blunting the glare of weapons' fire.

She saw Griffin—the largest of the team—focused, determined as he advanced. A weapon tucked to his shoulder. Back bent forward as he advanced. With him, Max.

Behind them, Canyon, walking backwards shooting. Firing. Calling counts.

Azzan.

Where was he?

Her heart sped up, keeping cadence with the popping of guns. The thump of concussions against her breastbone. A hole now gaped where the doors to the main ballroom once stood.

A shadow spirited through the smoke and dusty field. Sailed into the air.

Azzan! Her heart sailed with him. Saw his lanky but muscular build vanish into the thick cloud of smoke and haze.

"Perfect timing," a voice hissed in her ear. Pulling her straight.

"Let her go! Let her go!" Max shouted.

The three men formed up, advancing. Fury in their gaze. Intent in their postures. Bullets in their weapons.

A blade glinted in her periphery.

Everly drew in a sharp breath, realizing she was dead. Realizing she'd see Grandpa.

"Falling petals!" a shout proclaimed.

Even as the sweet words kissed her ears, Everly knew. Saw. Understood. She twisted and dropped, peering up at the ceiling as a form grew in the haze. Took shape. Grew intent. Brought violence.

Gunfire crackled.

Azzan crashed into the assassin with a meaty thump.

She felt the weight drop on her legs. Snatching her legs free, she curled in on herself, shielding. Praying.

Something latched onto her, dragged her. She whimpered, scared to find it was the assassin. Come to do as he had done to Grandpa.

"Everly. Everly!"

She turned, stunned to find the terrified eyes of Azzan peering down at her. A sob wrested free of her tight control. Leapt between them. He hauled her into his arms. Slipped an arm beneath her legs. Lifted her as he pushed to his feet.

Arms tight around his neck, Everly clung for dear life. Face pressed to his neck, she cried—not out of fear. Not out of terror. Not out of the nightmare that had too long held her. But because in a cliché-turned-beautiful, Azzan had been an assassin. But not against her life. Not against her hope. But against her fears.

"He's gone! Åkesson's gone!"

Confusion swirled and choked them. They rechecked the room, and Canyon sprinted toward the rear door.

Azzan twisted around, glanced where they'd last seen the assassin. Lights bloomed in the darkness out back. An engine rattled.

"Snowmobiles!"

"Stay with them," Azzan hissed at her.

"No!"

He sprinted to the wall. Hopped up. Toed it. Catapulted himself to the fireplace. Used the bricks for toe- and foot-holds. Then sprung at the beam. He swung. Swung harder. Up onto the beam.

Then he was running, full sprint at the window.

Holding her breath, shocked at what he was doing.

"He has to do this," Max said, coming alongside her. "If Åkesson escapes, he can come back. When you aren't as protected. Kill both of you."

Everly felt her chin bouncing. "Will he kill him?"

"If he has to," Max said. "Let's get you somewhere safe."

"Window," Azzan shouted as he ran full out at the glass. Terrified he'd hit that pane and break his neck, Everly barely noticed the team aiming weapons at the upper glass. They fired in unison. Breaking, weakening the pane.

Azzan dove through the air at the window.

CHAPTER 16

AZZAN LANDED CROOKEDLY, the bank of snow pitching him sideways. He came up in a crouch, attuning his senses to the noise, the cold. Aware he wasn't dressed for winter combat. Not caring. The snow was soft and slushy, melting, making every step difficult. A struggle. To the far right, near the end of the lodge, he saw the top of a large white delivery truck, mostly buried beneath the snow. Except the upper two feet. And the top, which now supported three snowmobiles.

Getaway.

Not if I can help it!

Azzan tried running, but it was a futile effort. Even as he heard one of the snowmobiles launch, he dove across several feet of icy padding and rolled again until he caught the lip of a balcony. He swung hand over hand until he reached the end, then swooped himself over to the next one. He toed it, and caught. Hoisted himself up. Just one more. Then the gap between the lodge and the truck.

A man was trying to get a second one to start, while a third aimed his machine wrong and went down, nose first. The revving engine screamed in defeat as Azzan swung his way over to the edge. Azzan pulled himself up, glancing toward the escaping Åkesson, the red light fading in the distance.

Move it! Azzan climbed onto the waist-high rail. Eyed the roofline. And threw himself at it, knowing the snow would devour him if he lost his grip.

He caught the edge.

Crack!

The roofline shuddered. Hard-packed snow and ice snapped against his hand. Shoved it free of its grip.

His body swung away. He dropped into the snowy abyss. Unless—

He flung himself around a full ninety degrees. Leaped for the last balcony. He clanged against it, far too close, yet not enough to land safely. Iron rang out and pain radiated through his hip. He ignored it and clambered over. Then hopped and jumped onto the other side.

Saw the second craft launch.

Azzan crouched on the rail. He wouldn't make it. Too far. But he wasn't going to stop. Had to try.

Wait. He eyed the siding. Saw variations. Crevices. It'd make his fingers bleed, but he wouldn't feel it, they were numb. He was numb. Spidering up onto the wall, he worked his way to the side, half watching the indentations, half eying the last attacker.

He had to get that machine. Only way to catch Åkesson. His left hand slipped, fingers numb and protesting the icy elements. Gritting his clattering teeth, he toed up and reached the corner.

The third machine roared off the truck.

Azzan brought his legs up, tucked tight, then shoved up, springboarding off and corkscrewing through the icy night, right at the gunman. He sighted him seconds before their shoulders collided. He felt the craft shudder beneath the guy, whose grip broke. They flipped.

Intent and surprise on his side, Azzan twisted around to find the gunman groaning, holding his shoulder as he came up, disoriented.

Azzan coldcocked him. Left the guy in the snow and shoved his way to the craft, still rattling its objection over being on its side. He shoved the snowmobile over and mounted it. Revved it, then let the brake release.

Air tore at him as he screamed across the mountain, homing in on the lone red light. The deafening roar of the storm and wind made it impossible to hear if he had help or trouble on his tail. But he had one goal: stop Åkesson.

The light grew, distance closing. Azzan's fury drove him harder. He kept his chin tucked and barreled on, reveling that he was—

Fire and pain seared across his arm.

He winced, glancing at the blaze of red above his elbow. Snapped his gaze up. Realized a mistake—he wasn't closing in on him. Åkesson had come about. They were headed right toward each other!

Sparks flew off the hull of his machine. Instead of swerving to avoid the bullets, Azzan simply lowered his chest to the hull. Kept his gaze trained on the enemy challenging him. Threatening him. He focused on what Åkesson had done to him—killed his mother. What Åkesson had done to Everly—killed her grandfather. He'd killed enough. Too many. Innocents. This mercenary needed a snow burial.

The shape grew closer. Closer. Bigger.

Azzan readied himself. Dug his toes in, to push off and have better traction. He slipped his hand to the weapon he'd tucked at the small of his back. He could tell by the way the mercenary was positioning himself that he planned to launch right at him. A colossal attack of assassins.

Let him think that.

Ten seconds.

Everly. This was for Everly.

Eight . . .

He had to kill this guy. Had to stop him. Or this would never end.

Four . . .

With the wash of lights and rooflines in sight, Azzan noted they were closer to the lodge than he realized. Was Åkesson coming back to finish Everly?

Not happening.

Azzan shoved upward.

Bullets whizzed and sparked off the machine.

He hit the right handle. Used his momentum to pitch it sideways.

Åkesson saw the move. Saw what Azzan intended.

Azzan flew away, spine to the lodge. Facing Åkesson. Firing.

Åkesson's machine nosed his in the side. The gas tank whistled. Then detonated.

Fire and the concussion of the small explosion pitched him backward.

He landed hard. Air punched from his lungs. He rolled onto all fours. Saw the mercenary on the ground. Not moving. Azzan scrambled, cringing at the pain in his arm and side. Threw himself at the guy.

Åkesson came alive with a howl, his shoulder bloodied. His face scraped. But his rage intact.

Azzan held the weapon on him. Right in his face.

The man stilled, hands winging out. In surrender. Feigned surrender.

Finger in the trigger well wasn't close enough for this guy. He eased it.

Heard a noise.

Åkesson grinned. "She's watching. Can you do it? Kill me? Be the thing she despises?"

Azzan hesitated. Swallowed. He couldn't. Not knowing she was there. But he also couldn't let this guy live. What options?

Like lighting, he struck. Slammed his fist into the guy's face with a cocktail of rage and futility. Åkesson went limp and Azzan pushed back onto his haunches, feet sinking into the snow. He shifted back. Tried to raise himself onto his feet.

A scream startled him.

He saw it—Åkesson, eyes closed, body still—except his shooting hand. It came up. Weapon aimed.

Crack!

A meaty thump sounded beneath him. He glanced down. Åkesson was missing a good chunk of his chest. Azzan stumbled back. Glanced to the lodge.

Max and Canyon were fighting their way to him.

Colton lay on the roof, in the snow, with his sniper rifle. In the room below his perch, Everly stood at the window.

Azzan dropped against the snowy blanket. Too cold, too numb. But he felt the warmth of her gaze. Seeping down his side and hip, the warmth of his blood.

EPILOGUE

Christmas Morning

THOUGH CANYON HAD stitched Azzan's bullet wound and given him a mega-dose of ibuprofen, Azzan felt the acute pain of two nights ago. Christmas carols drifted through the fire pit-warmed lodge as the children gathered around. Word had come on the handheld that the sheriff's department and Park Rangers were closing in on reaching them. The soft snow made it too treacherous to attempt a helicopter rescue.

"Hey," Griffin said, holding up a cup of eggnog. "To Marshall Vaughn."

"To the Kid," Max toasted.

"Hear, hear," Azzan, Canyon, and Colton chimed in.

"If the Kid were here," Griffin said, "I think he'd be making a play for your girl, Lygos."

Though surprise tugged at him, Azzan didn't object.

"Wait—what's this? Lygos isn't arguing about a girlfriend?"

"He never has a girlfriend."

"Okay, okay," Azzan said, shaking his head, all too aware of Everly looking over from where she stood by the buffet. "Just because you guys are jealous—"

"Whoa, no!" Max wrapped an arm around his wife. "You are not getting me in trouble with that line. I'm perfectly happy with my wife. No jealousy here."

"I think you know better than to turn this against me and my baby girl," Griffin said, arms coiling around his petite but deadly wife.

"Daddy," little Lyric said, "I thought I was your baby girl."

"Stepped in it, big guy," Griff's wife said.

"Man, y'all got sap running out your ears," Canyon taunted. "Dani knows how much I love her—"

"I think you'd better remind me, before you find yourself sleeping on a snow drift."

Griffin hooted, the banter continuing as the children sang and drank hot cocoa.

Azzan left the group and moseyed over to Everly, sitting with a very humbled Harden Frances, and the rest of her team. He held out a hand. Though she hesitated, Everly accepted it and came to her feet. He led her to a quiet spot. "Sorry about all that," Azzan whispered. "I know I didn't come clean with you. I was . . . afraid. Afraid you'd hate me. Hate what I am."

"What you were."

Azzan considered her. "Can I read into those words?"

Everly looked at him.

"It's Christmas, you know."

She frowned.

"Christmas miracles."

"You expecting one?" she asked with a smile.

"I'm hoping we're still friends." He held out a rose.

Everly hesitated. Swallowed.

"I know roses have been a bad omen to you for a long time." He breathed around the fear of rejection that lodged in his chest— right next to the healing wound. "I'm hoping this weekend changed that. Or at least, made it less terrible."

Everly stared at it. She twisted her lips, as if avoiding crying.

He winced. "Too early?"

She took it. Pressed it to her nose. "This," she said, nodding to the group laughing and singing Christmas songs. There weren't any presents since nobody expected to be here on Christmas Day. ". . . I've never had 'family' like this. And definitely not on Christmas morning. It's always one person yelling at another, or someone hung over because they hate the holidays and family gatherings."

Griffin belted out a jazz rendition of *God Rest Ye Merry Gentlemen* as he swooped Lyric into his arms. The others joined in.

"Tell me about your parents." Her question was soft, but laden with insistence. "That's where it began, right? This quest of yours for vengeance. What made you become an assassin."

Azzan lowered his head. Nodded it.

"Tell me."

"My parents loved each other. Deeply. But hard times forced them to return to my Palestinian grandparents." He clenched his jaw. "They hated my mother. Hated her simply for being Israeli. My father died—and I believe it was a sort of honor killing by one of his brothers, though I never found out which one—my mother and I had nowhere to go. Her family was dead. His family hated her. We lived in a small shack outside their beautiful home. One day, I was awakened by a . . . a thud." He swallowed, still able to hear it. Hear the sound of his mother's lifeless body hitting the dirt floor.

"They killed her."

Azzan couldn't face her. Couldn't look into her eyes.

But Everly framed his face with her hands, willing his gaze to hers.

"That's when it started. They told me Mossad killed her, a retaliation against her father—a Mossad operator. They recruited me, used me to steal secrets from my grandfather's family. But I got caught."

"By the Israelis."

He nodded. "Best mistake I ever made. They brought me in, educated me. Showed me proof that the Palestinians had killed my mother. Hired an assassin to make it look like it was her family."

"Åkesson."

"Yes. I hunted him down. Found him. And failed."

Everly stared at him. Smiled.

How could she smile? "What?"

"He wanted us both dead, yet he is the one gone."

It was too good to be true.

Not the violence. Not the attack on innocent lives. They were all to be grieved. Nightshade had averted the wrong done. Settled it. Ended it. But the way Everly had looked at him after he'd extricated himself from the team neutralizing Åkesson . . . The way she looked at him now.

You're misreading this.

But he wasn't. His training taught him how to discern the difference. "I am not that man anymore, Evvy."

She breathed a smile. "I know."

He could never have hoped. Never dreamed.

Azzan bent closer. "I . . . is it too soon to say I love you?"

"You're two days late," she teased as he pressed his lips to hers.

Whistles and catcalls shot up.

"Get a room!"

"They can't do that until they're married!"

"Then get a preacher!"

ABOUT THE AUTHOR

Ronie Kendig is an award-winning, bestselling author of over twenty novels. She and her veteran husband live in beautiful Northern Virginia with their children and retired military working dog, VVolt N629 (ret). Ronie's degree in psychology has helped her pen novels of intense, raw characters.

To learn more about Ronie Kendig, visit her online!
Website: www.roniekendig.com
Facebook (facebook.com/rapidfirefiction)
Twitter (@roniekendig)
Goodreads (goodreads.com/RonieK)
Pinterest (pinterest.com/roniek/)
Instagram (@kendigronie)

MORE
RAPID-FIRE FICTION
FROM
RONIE KENDIG

THE DISCARDED HEROES

*Currently out-of-print; soon to be re-released

Nightshade
DISCARDED HEROES #1

After a tour of duty in a war-torn country, embattled former Navy SEAL Max Jacobs finds himself discarded and alienated from those he loves as he struggles with combat-related PTSD.

Digitalis
DISCARDED HEROES #2

Colton Neeley left his military career to take care of his four-year old daughter. Although he's firm in his faith now, the repercussions of his former life are still evident—namely in the form of his daughter and his debilitating flashbacks from combat-related trauma.

*Wolfsbane**
DISCARDED HEROES #3

Haunted by memories of a mission gone bad, former Green Beret Canyon Metcalfe wrestles with misgivings and growing feelings for a senator's daughter embroiled in a nightmare. Setting aside his hesitation, he and Nightshade unravel lethal secrets.

*Firethorn**
DISCARDED HEROES #4

Former Marine and current Nightshade team member Griffin "Legend" Riddell is comfortable. So comfortable he never sees the set up that lands him in a maximum security prison, charged with murder. How can he prove his innocence behind bars?

THE TOX FILES

The Warrior's Seal
THE TOX FILES prequel novella

Special Forces operative Cole "Tox" Russell and his team are tasked in a search-and-rescue—the U.S. president has been kidnapped during a goodwill tour. The mission nosedives when an ancient biblical artifact and a deadly toxin wipe out villages. Tox must stop the terrorists and the toxin to save the president.

Conspiracy of Silence
THE TOX FILES #1

Four years after a tragic mission decimated his career and his team, Cole "Tox" Russell is *persona non grata* to the United States. And that's fine—he just wants to be left alone. But when a dormant, centuries-old disease is unleashed, Tox is lured back into action.

Crown of Souls
THE TOX FILES #2

Six months after stopping a deadly plague, Cole "Tox" Russell and his team are enjoying a little rest. That peace is short-lived when Tox is hit by a sniper shot. The enemy is one of their own, a rogue Special Forces team operator.

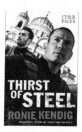

Thirst of Steel
THE TOX FILES #3 (July 2018)

Dismantled centuries ago, the sword of Goliath is still rumored to thirst for its enemies' blood. Cole "Tox" Russell only wants to begin his life with Haven Cortes, but he must first complete a final mission: retrieve that sword and destroy the deadly Arrow & Flame Order.

THE QUIET PROFESSIONALS

Raptor 6
QUIET PROFESSIONALS #1

Captain Dean Watters keeps his mission and his team in the forefront of his laser-like focus. So when Dean's mission and team are threatened, his Special Forces training kicks into high gear. Failing to stop hackers from stealing national security secrets from the military's secure computers and networks isn't an option.

Hawk
QUIET PROFESSIONALS #2

Raptor's communications expert, Staff Sergeant Brian "Hawk" Bledsoe, is struggling with his inner demons, leaving him on the verge of an "other than honorable" discharge. Plagued with corrupted intel, Raptor team continues to track down the terrorist playing chess with their lives.

Falcon
QUIET PROFESSIONALS #3

Special Forces operator Salvatore "Falcon" Russo vowed to never again speak to or trust Lieutenant Cassandra Walker after a tragedy four years ago. But as Raptor closes in on the cyber terrorists responsible for killing two of their own, Sal must put his life—and the lives of his teammates—in her hands.

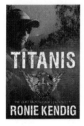

Titanis
QUIET PROFESSIONALS #4

Eamon "Titanis" Straider left the military and civilization behind after betrayal cost the life of a teammate. Living on this super yacht, the ViCross, Eamon reluctantly agrees to host an event for his parents, who are part of the Australian political machine. When an attractive woman arrives with his mother, Eamon is furious—and determined to find out what she is hiding.

A BREED APART

Trinity: Military War Dog
A BREED APART #1

A year ago in Afghanistan, Green Beret Heath Daniel's career was destroyed. Along with his faith. Now he and his military war dog, Trinity train other dogs and their handlers through the A Breed Apart organization. The job works. But his passion is to be back in the field.

Talon: Combat Tracking Team
A BREED APART #2

All Air Force veteran Aspen Courtland wants is her brother back. The US Marine Corps says he's dead, but Aspen won't believe it till she sees his body. Her only hope is her brother's tracking dog, Talon, but a brutal attack has left the dog afraid of his own shadow.

Beowulf: Explosives Detection Dog
A BREED APART #3

Former Navy handler Timbrel Hogan has more attitude than her Explosives Detection Dog, Beowulf, but she's a tough woman who gets the job done. Green Beret Tony "Candyman" VanAllen likes a challenge and convincing the hard-hitting handler they belong together might just get him killed. When tragedy strikes and Tony's career is jeopardized, Timbrel must re-evaluate her life and priorities—and fast.

ABIASSA'S FIRE FANTASY SERIES

Embers
ABIASSA'S FIRE #1

HE'S COMING FOR THEM. AND THE KINGDOM. Haegan and Kaelyria Celahar are royal heirs of the Nine Kingdoms, but Haegan is physically crippled. What chance does he have against Poired Dyrth, the greatest enemy the kingdom has ever faced, who wields fire with a power none can match?

Accelerant
ABIASSA'S FIRE #2

The Nine Kingdoms bleed. Leaderless, ravaged, the land desperately awaits deliverance from Poired Dyrth's devastating campaign. But what if one blight can only be cleansed by another?

The promised Fierian is known by many names. Judge. Destroyer. Scourge. And now one other: Haegan, Prince of Seultrie. Once a cripple, now a gifted Accelerant, Haegan can no longer run from the truth.

Fierian
ABIASSA'S FIRE #3 (March 2018)

Abiassa's people fall. Her Fierian dwindles. Her Deliverers wait as Poired Dyrth marches unchecked through the Nine Kingdoms. He's taken the Embers of countless Accelerants. He's taken Zaethien and Hetaera, the mightiest of the Nine's cities. He's taken the blood of the royal family. Now Dyrth is after Haegan's power—the Fierian's power. And after that, he wants the world.

OPERATION ZULU REDEMPTION

Operation Zulu Redemption

They never should've existed. Now they don't.

In the aftermath of their first highly successful op, the first all-female special ops team, known as Zulu, discovered that innocent civilians—women and children—died at their hands. Zulu was set up to take the devastating fall. Fearing for their lives, the Zulu team vanished.

DEAD RECKONING

Dead Reckoning

A Rapid-Fire Rewrite–Expanded & Updated–14,000 new words!

A deadly encounter in the Arabian Sea becomes a fight for her life!

Underwater archaeologist Shiloh Blake finds herself in the middle of an international nuclear arms clash during her first large-scale dig and flees for her life. She doesn't know who to trust or how to stay alive.

Want the latest Rapid-Fire intel on upcoming releases and events? Then become a recruit and join up. Start with my newsletter, then track me down on social media: Goodreads, Facebook, Instagram, and Twitter!

Excitement is contagious! The more reviews a book has, the more likely other readers are to find it. Please consider posting a review or rating to help Rapid-Fire Fiction gain a louder voice and audience.

Made in the USA
Middletown, DE
24 May 2018